This one is for Judy and her very own heroes.

RANCHER UNDER THE GUN

BARB HAN

TORJAKE PUBLISHING

Editing: Ali Williams

Cover Design: Jacob's Cover Designs

1

This wasn't how Daphne Lynn Thompson imagined herself returning to Lone Star Pass after a decade, as a divorced single mother. In her mind, the family property was still in pristine condition, her father was his same onery self and not suffering from rapid onset dementia, and jars of honey still flew off the shelves of the small family business.

Daphne stood on the front porch, hesitating a moment before going inside. Her nine-year-old son Henry stood beside her along with Luis and Luna, their two-year-old Dobermans. The thought of facing her father again before she had time to process his diagnosis kept her from going in. The thought of seeing the scared, confused look in his eyes —even if it only lasted a flash—rooted her feet to the aging wooden porch.

"Is this where you grew up, Momma?" Henry's eyes widened with pure excitement and wonder as he looked around at the expansive yard.

"It is," Daphne said, tousling the hair on top of his head. He was the spitting image of his father, younger with a sweeter face. "And I loved every minute of it." Well, almost every minute, right up until the end when she'd had to leave town and break her high school boyfriend's heart.

"Can I show Luis and Luna around?" Henry practically jumped up and down, barely able to contain himself. She wished for half of his energy. "Pl-e-e-e-ease?"

Daphne scanned the area. Very few people knew she was coming home, and word couldn't possibly have gotten around this fast so he should be safe to roam freely as long as the dogs were with him.

"Stay inside the fenced yard and where you can see the house at all times," she warned with a finger wag. At twenty-eight years old, the move basically turned her into an old schoolmarm. She put the finger away, tucking her hand inside the pocket of her slacks instead. "Don't go anywhere near the pond, okay?"

His eyes lit up at the mention of water nearby. He'd always been a water baby just like her. She could almost see the ideas forming in his little brain.

Bending down to his level and raising his chin up until his eyes met hers, she said, "No arguments. If I catch you near the pond, you'll be in big trouble with me, mister." Henry had always been a dream child. She figured the rebellion would kick in some day—a day she hoped was far off in the future—and he would be more than a handful to make up for the fact he'd been pretty much the perfect child so far.

Having him look her in the eyes ensured he was listening, and not already so busy plotting out his adventures that he'd lost his ability to hear her. He had a great imagination and was a little too used to alone time. Guilt stabbed her for the fact her son had spent so much time with only her and the dogs for companionship, with too few playdates for the past two years. At his tender age, did he even remember the last time a friend had slept over? Even though being hidden the last two years was for his own protection, it seemed wholly unfair to do to a kid. Since there'd been no choice, she decided to cut herself a little slack.

"Promise me you'll stick close to the house?" she urged.

"I won't go near the pond," Henry said with about as much enthusiasm as if she'd asked him to eat an entire bowl of broccoli.

"Thank you," she said. Before she got the words out, Henry was hopping off the porch and calling for his dogs. "Or the hives."

He practically beamed at the last word. "I want to see the bees. They won't hurt me."

"They don't normally sting. Only when they feel threatened, but you shouldn't go see them without me," she said. The beekeeper had promised to stay on part-time, which would help with the transition. Plus, his wife had been pitching in to help out with the store. Daphne owed the Schmidts for being willing to stick around, even though the business was barely able to make payroll and the writing on the wall suggested that it wouldn't be able to for much longer. The state of the family business was another shocker.

"One more thing. Come inside if anyone pulls into the drive. Got it?" she shouted after him. The bright orange U-Haul filled with their belongings stood sentinel in the driveway. Her late-model Jeep attached to the back. Daphne didn't want to think about how hers and Henry's entire lives were able to fit inside a 10-foot truck.

Her son did an immediate about face, hopped back on the porch and ran straight into her, wrapping his little arms around her waist and hugging her tightly. They'd done okay together just the two of them hiding out in Dallas, right? The smile on his face made her think so.

"When can we go see the bees?" Henry's eyes lit up when he asked about them.

"Later. I promise. For now, don't go anywhere near them without me," she warned. "But I'll take you to see the apiary after I say hello to Pops."

Henry hugged her even tighter. The excitement in his body hummed like a live wire. He'd been talking about them nonstop since learning they were coming back to her childhood home.

When Henry let go, he said, "Pinky swear that if a car comes, I'll run straight into Grandpa's house." He adorably brought up his right hand and then wiggled his pinky at her along with a beaming smile. She wished time would stand still and Henry would stop growing. How had nine years gone by so fast?

She linked pinkies and 'shook' to seal the deal. Henry took off, hopping off the porch in search of adventure a few seconds later. A boy and his dogs. Luis and Luna wouldn't let anyone get close to Henry, she reminded herself as her pulse kicked up a few notches at the thought of him wandering the five-acre property. It was silly, she knew, because she'd grown up here and this was one of least crime-ridden places she could think of. But the person out for her and Henry didn't fall into a general crime bucket.

On a sharp intake of air meant for courage, Daphne reached for the knob then opened the door. "Dad?"

"In the kitchen," he said. Edward Owen Thompson was the proud owner of Beekeeper Honey and had been the sole proprietor since before Daphne had been born. The place had been in the family four generations and gave her a connection to the grandparents she'd only known through stories. She'd grown up running through the meadow on the south lawn and taking her canoe out on the pond with her best friend by her side. Hers had been an idyllic childhood, filled with innocence until life turned upside down and she grew up real quick. But she didn't want to think about the past right now when the future stared her in the face.

As she walked across the creaky wood floors, she took note of the fact not much had changed here in the past decade. The same plaid couch sat to one side of the room, across from a flatscreen TV that looked relatively new. Her dad's recliner aimed directly at the TV. The same coffee table, a relic from the 70s with the stains and marks to prove it, sat in front of the sofa. The décor was minimal and there must be half an inch of dust on the bookshelves her dad had made for her. Those definitely stayed but the couch with its sunken in cushions needed to go.

An alarm company was first on the docket, though.

Dad sat at the kitchen table reading the paper and drinking a cup of coffee like she'd seen him do hundreds, if not thousands, of times before. There was comfort in seeing something so familiar when her world was about to be turned upside down again.

"Hey, Dad," she said, walking straight to him and giving him a hug.

"Today's the big day," he said after a warm embrace. Relief washed over her when he answered and seemed to be himself. The doctor said these moments of clarity would peter out in the coming months and she planned to hold tight to them as long as they were here.

"Moving day is here." She had made the decision to quit her job and pack up her small north Dallas apartment in a matter of days. Always being ready to move, and more importantly ready to leave with little to no notice, had been her life for the past twenty-four-plus months. The thought of sticking around in one place both scared and excited her. For the first time in a decade, she was home. The only thing missing was her best friend Ian Firebrand. The two of them had been inseparable by high school, dating by junior year, and full-fledged-with-no-going-back-in-love by graduation. She'd been told it was nothing more than an infatuation that time would make disappear from her thoughts altogether. And yet, even when she was a young and naïve eighteen-year-old, she'd known that couldn't be true. Thinking about him now caused her pulse to rise and her heart to hammer the inside of her ribs despite having no contact since she'd left town.

"Coffee is fresh," Dad said, motioning toward the machine. His expression was a mix of happy and concern. She could identify with both. Being here with him stirred up so many good memories. Like breakfasts here at the table every morning before school and doing homework while he watched TV in the adjacent room. Then there was dancing around the kitchen while standing on his feet when she'd been in grade school. Hot tears burned the backs of her eyes. She blinked a couple of times and refocused.

"The smell hit me when I first walked in," she said. Moving to the coffee machine, she located a mug and filled it. Taking in a deep breath, she let the smell of dark roast fill her senses. The scent was familiar and brought her back to the days of Ian picking her up before class. He'd always get here early for a cup of coffee with her dad before school. The minute the two of them got inside his truck, he would lean over and kiss her, the taste of dark roast still on his lips.

Daphne took in a sharp breath, trying to ease the pain that also came from remembering. Besides, a piece of Ian had been with her for the past ten years. Being home reminded her of all the other good times she'd blocked out for survival's sake. Because leaving Ian and shutting off all communication in the process had been the single most difficult thing she'd ever done.

The thought of running into him again practically gutted her. Forget about the fact that it would be impossible to continue to hide Henry from his father.

IAN FIREBRAND SAT on the farm road with his left blinker on. There was little traffic on this road, and none at the moment, so he had time to consider whether or not it was a good idea to honor Mr. Thompson's request to help move some heavy furniture and boxes. In ten years, Ian had never once turned the older man down when he needed something. The thought of doing so now made Ian feel like a class-A jerk.

But this situation was complicated.

The rhythmic clicks of the blinker reminded Ian he needed to make a choice. Turn left, drive up the gravel road that led to Mr. Thompson's home, and take a chance of seeing Daphne again. She'd been gone for ten years, taking a piece of his heart along with her. They'd been young and stupid and, he'd thought, hopelessly in love. His grandfather, the Marshall as they called him, had warned Ian that Daphne would wake up and leave him someday. His fool heart had believed the love between the two of them was real and could last forever. That the two of them could defy the odds and be the two percent that made the long haul.

Apparently, all it had taken was graduation for her to wake up and realize she was done. Ian was still scratching his head over why she'd decided to leave him and shatter his heart. Her flimsy excuse of needing to see the world before she settled down, and not being able to if the two of them stayed in contact, didn't make any more sense back then than it did now.

Daphne was married and in bad shape. That was all Ian's brother Grayson had said the last time the two of them spoke. She was moving back to live with her father and Mr. Thompson requested Ian's help to move a few things before his daughter arrived with her 'junk' as he'd called it. There'd been a mix of joy and something that sounded a whole lot like resignation in Mr. Thompson's voice, which had caused all kinds of questions to form in Ian's mind about just how bad off Daphne must be. Since he didn't exactly want to pull up a ringside seat to someone else's pain, he sat there. *Click. Clock. Click. Clock.*

Ian issued a sharp sigh. He was a man of his word and he'd promised to help Mr. Thompson, just as he'd done dozens of times in the past when the old man had needed a hand. This time shouldn't be any different, no matter who might end up under the same roof. Being in the house would be temporary. Ian would get in and get out. Depending on how big the job was, he could call for reinforcements. Normally, Mr. Thompson's requests took less than an hour. Ian had cleared his day for this one, just in case.

The only thing Ian didn't do was get near the bees. Thankfully, they were kept on the back portion of the property far enough away to never be a problem. And Ian would know having spent most of his childhood running around the property with Daphne.

Touching his foot to the gas pedal, Ian turned left and onto the gravel road. He maintained a slow, steady pace until he hit Mr. Thompson's turnoff. The small winding path opened up to a view of the house, property, and a U-Haul. Ian bit back a curse. He had half a mind to turn around and drive off rather than pull up beside what had to be Daphne's moving truck.

The thought of running into her and her husband sent a lead fireball raging through his chest. He couldn't picture Daphne married to anyone else, but...

Ian stopped himself right there. He'd dated plenty of women over the years and had been in several relationships. Of course, Daphne had moved on, as had he—once he'd stopped licking his wounds over the breakup. The worse part of the whole situation was that he'd been blindsided. One minute, they'd been happy as a lark. The next, she was moving to Austin to start a new life away from him so she could 'find' herself and see the world.

Thinking back brought up all the pain and frustration as though it had happened yesterday. Ian parked next to the U-Haul, blocking his view of the old farmhouse. He'd offered to bring over a couple buckets of paint and spruce the place up, but Mr. Thompson could be stubborn when it came to accepting help, taking only the minimum needed in order to get by.

Ian put the ignition in park but stopped short of cutting off the engine. The urge to back out of the spot and retrace the drive was a physical force. The idea of seeing Daphne again when it had been so easy for her to leave felt like he'd been crushed and sat heavy on his chest.

Maybe it was time to walk inside that house and finally get closure. Seeing Daphne wearing a wedding ring would do the trick. As far as he knew, she had a couple of kids by now. The thought sent a cold shiver racing down his back. *Get used to it,* he thought. Daphne was here and would most likely have a family by now. Grayson's comment about her being in bad shape had kept Ian from sleeping a couple of nights since hearing the news. What if she'd been or still was in an abusive relationship. No matter how they'd left things those old protective feelings kicked up. Right, wrong, or indifferent, the thought of anyone hurting her caused his hands to fist. The thought of seeing her again at all was a gut punch.

Rather than let his mind take off into unwanted territory, he turned off his truck and exited the vehicle. He rounded the U-Haul in time to hear the front door opening and Daphne running onto the creaky wooden porch. Shock didn't begin to describe the feeling of seeing her again. So much so, it rooted him to his spot. There she stood all five-feet-four-inches of her with that long, wavy blonde hair and full, thick lips on a heart-shaped face.

She waved her hands wildly at him. Her concerned expression stopped him in his tracks. It only took a second to realize why. From the corner of his eye, he saw two massive Dobermans gunning toward him.

"Are they friendly?" he asked, putting his hands up, palms out in the surrender position.

Daphne spouted a command in another language. German? The Dobermans stopped and immediately sat, but it was the sandy-haired boy catching up to them who caught Ian's attention. His experience around kids was limited to kiddos under the age of two, so he had no idea how old this boy was.

"They will be now, unless I tell them otherwise," Daphne warned. His heart took a serious hit at seeing her again, like a sucker punch to the solar plexus that knocked all the air out of his lungs. Ian struggled to take in a breath as a whole bunch of memories came crashing down on him.

There Daphne stood, slightly older but no less beautiful. In fact, she was even more stunning than he remembered. He'd regretted deleting all those pictures of her that she'd insisted on taking on his phone. After she'd left, he half convinced himself she would be back. Days passed with no word and then weeks. A month came and went, then two. At the year mark, he'd gone into a fit and removed everything that reminded him of Daphne. Later, he regretted the move since he had no memories of the good times to look back on.

An odd feeling overtook him as he glanced over at the Dobermans. It registered that these were no ordinary house pets. These were trained guard dogs. "Does this have something to do with the trouble you're in?"

"Who said I was in trouble?" she asked a little too quickly. The defensiveness in her voice said he was on the right track. Even now after all these years, he could read her tone.

"Stay with Luis and Luna, Henry," she shouted to the boy. He was far enough away that Ian couldn't make out the details of his face, but he seemed familiar. Of course, he decided, Daphne's son would be familiar because he was part of her.

"I'd like to meet your son," he said to a frightened-looking Daphne. What was that all about? "How old is he, by the way?"

Ian couldn't pinpoint why it was suddenly so important to him to be introduced to the boy. Then there was Daphne's reaction to Ian being there in the first place. His thoughts were bouncing around, then his mind snapped to the worst possible scenario. The one that said her jealous husband was lurking nearby and she was scared to death he would see Ian.

Except it didn't make sense that her father would invite

him here to help if that was the case. No. Something else was going on.

There she stood on the porch, looking far too fine for his heart's good. She'd stopped growing at five-feet-four-inches a long time ago and she'd filled out with enough curves to be sexy. She still had those full pouty lips with the most kissable cupid's bow. Even from this distance he could see the blue of her eyes. Her hair was longer and thicker now, and the same sandy-blonde as her son's, from what Ian could tell at this distance.

Daphne stood there for a long moment with her arms folded over her chest. The metal of her gold wedding band glinted in the sunlight and had the same effect of burning his eyes. He should have expected this on some level but had no idea the amount of heartache that had been bubbling underneath the surface, still fresh and raw.

"Henry is nine and a half years old, Ian," she said, her gaze narrowing and her lips thinning.

Last time he checked, it took nine months for a baby to cook inside its mother, which meant...

"Does that mean what I think it does?" Ian asked, his gaze bouncing from the child to Daphne and back as a feeling of being completely dumbfounded struck like stray lightning in a blue sky.

She gave an almost imperceptible nod along with another warning shot. Ian got it. The kid within shouting distance and, clearly, he had no idea his father had just shown up. *His father.* Those words would haunt Ian. He had a son.

For a long moment, he stood there. It was like time warped and Ian got caught in the wave.

He was a father.

2

Daphne had known this day was a long time in the making. This wasn't how she'd pictured it going down. The hurt look on Ian's face would haunt her for a very long time to come and the ache in her chest was as raw as it had been the day she'd left town without looking back. She deserved the pain of seeing him again on some level, even though he had no idea the circumstances that led to her leaving town while pregnant with his child. The threat.

"I'm sorry, Ian," was all she could manage to say. "I really am."

He stood there, looking like he couldn't decide whether or not to walk in the house or bolt.

"How could you?" came out through clenched teeth.

"I promise to tell you everything you want to know as long as he's not within earshot." She nodded toward Henry, who was petting his dogs, blissfully unaware of the fact his life was about to change forever. Hers was too. She would be naïve to think otherwise. Based on the look in Ian's eyes, he intended to be part of Henry's life. Part of her was thrilled.

There'd been more days and nights than she could count that she'd wished Henry would be able to get to know his father. The thought of splitting holidays didn't feel as great.

"Momma, I can't get Luis or Luna to move," Henry complained as he wrapped both arms around Luna's neck and used all of the might of his slight frame as leverage to try to get the eighty-pound dog to budge. He abruptly shifted when that didn't work, locating a stick and throwing it as far as he could. Luna was well trained even at two years old.

"Do I have your agreement?" she asked Ian with a pleading look.

He gave a begrudging nod.

"Thank you," she said, dropping her arms and then twisting the gold band on the third finger of her left hand. She caught herself in the middle of the subconscious move. She gave the dogs a command to relax and then looked at Ian. "Mind if I ask what you're doing here?" It couldn't be to welcome her home after the way she'd left things. Daphne had many regrets in life but Ian wasn't one of them, despite her heart shattering into a thousand flecks of dust when she'd been forced to leave town and cut off communication.

"Your father invited me," he said absently, his full attention turned toward Henry as he loped off with his best friends after Daphne gave the relax command.

She needed to have a serious conversation with her dad and with Ian, in not necessarily that order. She'd known she would run into Ian at some point now that she was going to be living here. What she hadn't expected was for her own father to be the one to invite him over on day one, before she had a chance to get her bearings or figure out how she was going to introduce the man to his son. Then again, her father had no idea who Henry's father was. She'd disappeared from his life for a time too.

How stupid had she been to think she could live here again without the past coming to light or drawing attention?

"He's waiting in the kitchen," she said before turning around and heading back inside. It seemed the only way to distract Ian from watching his son.

The door hadn't closed behind her when it swung open again. She could feel Ian's masculine presence right behind her. He had the same effect on her that he'd had ten years ago, causing her body to warm and her face to flush. He'd filled out his six-feet-four-inch frame with ripples of muscles. His hair was shorter now and a little bit darker despite a few sun-kissed streaks. He'd always had an intensity about him but he was even more so now. And damned if he didn't look even better with his golden skin. He had the same chiseled from granite jawline and warm brown eyes as before. His face had a little more scruff that only proved to be sexy on him. Most women would consider him drop-dead gorgeous and she wouldn't argue against their point.

"Ian, you're here early," Daphne's father said after Ian followed her into the kitchen. He walked over and shook her father's outstretched hand. "Coffee is in the usual place. Make yourself at home."

Usual place? Her father made it seem like Ian came here all the time. How was that even possible? He'd certainly never mentioned the visits to her. But then, a lot had gone on in her life over the past decade and she'd specifically asked her dad not to mention Ian when she called. Somehow, she believed Ian would have cut off contact with her father. The fact they still had a relationship caught her off guard.

"Do you come visit my dad often?" Daphne asked

without making eye contact. She'd stopped and turned around at the farthest point in the room from the table, blocking out all the memories of the three of them sitting at the breakfast table of their eat-in kitchen. There'd been dinners too. It had taken Daphne all of junior year to figure out why Ian would come to her house for sandwiches or TV dinners, when his mother cooked from scratch every night. She'd confronted him in a teasing manner on the last night of school before summer break, and he'd finally come clean...*her.*

Ian walked over to the machine, located a mug, and poured himself a cup like he'd done it dozens of times.

"Every week," Dad said with a hint of pride. The news shocked her beyond belief.

"You never mentioned him," she said.

"Didn't see the need to," her father said. He was and had always been a man of few words. All of senior year when her and Ian became an official couple, her father had practically beamed. He'd casually mentioned on more than one occasion that Ian was exactly the kind of son he should have had. Her dad loved her more than words but if he'd been blessed with a son, he'd wanted it to be someone like Ian. "Except during calving season. Then, it's every other."

"Really?" she asked before she could rein the question in. First of all, the fact Ian visited her father after the way she'd left things caused her heart to squeeze. But then, the notion he still came by during calving season threatened to buckle her knees. For cattle ranchers, calving season was 'go time' when they barely slept at all. Back when they were teenagers, Ian would bring her home from school on a Friday night and fall asleep sitting at the table.

The fact he still cared about her father brought burning hot tears to the backs of her eyes. She gave herself permission to check his ring finger. Relief she had no right to own washed over her when she saw there was no gold band. Before she got too excited, she reminded herself not every married man wore a ring, especially ones who had outdoor jobs like Ian. Plus, just because he might not be married didn't mean he wasn't in a relationship.

A small and growing part of her argued no woman in the world was saint enough to allow her serious boyfriend or husband to regularly check on the father of his ex-girlfriend. Except a decade was a long time. Feelings changed. Based on the glare in Ian's eyes when he looked at her, his had turned to anger.

Who could blame him? Now, learning that he had a child gave him even more reason to hate her.

Ian stared at her dad for a long moment. The reason occurred to her. He wanted to know if her dad knew Henry belonged to him.

A new urgency to have a sit-down conversation with Ian filled her. "Maybe we should step onto the back porch where I can keep an eye on Henry while we talk."

The look Ian gave her would melt a glacier during an Alaskan winter.

"Nothing to discuss on my end. Besides, we're burning daylight and it seems I was asked to be here to help unload that U-Haul," he said, taking a sip of coffee before setting the mug down on the counter. "Might as well get to it."

"Right then. Thank you for coming," Dad said to Ian as he stood up. "I don't intend to waste your time."

"I'll help, Dad," Daphne interrupted. "You stay here and finish your coffee."

Dad waved her off. It would be just like him to feel responsible for unloading her U-Haul. At least he'd reached out for help.

"I can have half a dozen men here in half an hour," Ian offered, clearly on the same page as her about not asking her father to lift a finger. "Figure out how you want the living room arranged. Mark the pieces that need to go and I'll take care of the rest."

"Are you sure?" Dad asked, seeming to know he was no match for the contents of the U-Haul. Thank heaven for small miracles. The diagnosis had clearly shaken him up if he was backtracking on lifting heavy furniture. To be fair, she hadn't brought a whole lot with her. She didn't *own* much. But she wanted to hold onto the few pieces she'd collected to give Henry a sense of home no matter where they ended up living. The family home wasn't somewhere she'd expected to land and yet she couldn't deny how right it felt in a part of her to be here right now with her father and Ian like old times.

And that was where it ended because there was no going back.

THE EARLY SEPTEMBER Texas heat had nothing on the burning hot fire raging inside Ian. First, he had to find out that Daphne was back the hard way. Then, he saw the wedding band, which shouldn't bother him after a decade. Finally, he learned he was a father to a nine-year-old boy. *A father.*

There was no excuse in the world that could make him forgive Daphne for keeping his son from him for nine-freak-ing-years. However, now that Ian knew, he intended to get to know the boy and be in his life for the long haul from here on out.

After fishing his cell phone out of his front pocket, he

started to fire off a request for help in the family's group chat and then stopped himself mid-type. Bringing his brothers here, no matter how decent their intentions might be, could add pressure to an already tense situation. They would no doubt pick up on the fact that Henry was a Firebrand, and there would be questions Ian didn't have answers to. The chaos might be hard on Henry and Ian didn't want his son to meet the Firebrand side of family in this manner. Besides, he was still adjusting to the news.

A few deep breaths later, he tucked his cell back inside his pocket and walked over to the U-Haul. He released the lever and then opened the door as Henry played with the dogs on the opposite side of the house. The kid looked healthy and seemed happy. There were two positives.

"I'm sorry, for what it's worth," Daphne said from a few feet behind him.

Ian whirled around on her bringing up hell with him. "You don't get to apologize or try to gain sympathy in any form after keeping him from me all these years, Daphne. And shouldn't your husband be here doing this instead of it being me and your father?"

Daphne winced with each word like she was taking physical blows. He reminded his fool heart this wasn't the time to feel sorry for her despite the fact it seemed determined not to listen. What she'd done was wrong on every level.

"He isn't...I'm not..."

She ducked her head like she didn't want him to see the flood of tears trying to break free and roll down her cheeks. Ian bit back a string of curses.

"We'll run out of daylight if we don't get to work," he said lamely. Despite the shell-shocking news, he didn't want to make her cry. He had cared about her deeply at one time in his life and didn't have it in his heart to be a jerk.

After a sniffle and a cough that was probably meant to cover her emotions, she shook her head like she could shake off her feelings before closing the distance to the truck. She didn't look up or make eye contact as she passed him, and he tried to convince himself it was probably for the best. Looking into her eyes at this close range would most likely gut him anyway. He needed that like he needed a hole in the head.

Each grabbed individual boxes, lamps, and anything that could be carried on its own. He shifted the rest of the contents of the U-Haul to the back once they finished with the light, easy belongings. She'd packed correctly, shoving the heavy pieces in first.

There wasn't much here for a family of three. No table and chairs or dressers. No stacks of boxes with clothes or toys. Of course, the house already had plenty of furniture. She'd brought a cream-colored sofa with a matching chair. The fabric was good, and the pieces seemed comfortable enough. These must be replacements for the 70s plaid couch Mr. Thompson had kept around. The sofa had been uncomfortable ten years ago and would have only gotten worse with age. Ian remembered trying to kiss Daphne goodnight after her dad left the room only to find a wire poking him in the back when he'd tried to shift positions.

Maybe keeping the sofa had been a smart move for her father after all, Ian thought with a smile despite his heavy mood. If he ever had a daughter, he wanted one of those. *A daughter?* Ian was losing his mind. He was already in over his head with the surprise son.

As he headed out to the truck for one of the big pieces, he stopped on the porch and stared at Henry. Ian's mind was blown that he had a kid, let alone a nine-year-old. They'd lost a lot of time that could never be made up. Would the boy even like Ian? A bout of nerves struck at the thought.

Watching the kid play also sent an unfamiliar warmth straight to Ian's heart. He was in no way ready for marriage and kids, but it seemed, once again, life had other plans. At least on the kid part of the equation. It was hard to be angry about anything when he looked at Henry. He looked happy and well-adjusted. Ian had no plans to disrupt the kid's childhood. He did, however, want to figure out a way to ease into Henry's life. Too fast might shock the kid. Deliver the news too slow and Henry might feel betrayed. It was strange to wonder if his own son would even like him.

Daphne practically blew past him, her shoulder grazing his side. She was a good foot shorter than him, and always had been. Were the curves a result of having their child? Because she was even sexier than before with them, and those were thoughts that had no business in his mind while she was still wearing a wedding ring.

Ian refocused, watching her struggle with taking the chair out of the truck on her own. "I'd be happy to help with that."

"No, thanks," she quipped.

"Seriously, you'll strain your back if you try to pick it up like that." He jogged over and took the other side. "This will go a whole lot better if we work together."

Ian bit back the irony in those words, not ready to concede them to their personal lives as well. Right now, all he could focus on was his anger and the sense of betrayal that threatened to consume him from the inside out.

"Fine. I got my side," she said, gripping the bottom of the chair.

He took the opposite side, keeping low to accommodate

the height difference. "I'll go backwards. Just warn me when I need to take a step."

"Okay," Daphne said. A few steps later, the warning came.

Ian took one step, bearing most of the weight of the chair on his side so it wouldn't get even heavier for her. When he'd volunteered to walk backwards, he hadn't taken into account the fact he'd go up the stairs first. There was no reason for her to shoulder all the weight on her own.

"Watch your hands," she warned as he took a step into the doorway. He shifted his grip just in time to avoid nailing the doorframe.

"Thank you," he managed to get out begrudgingly.

After the chair, they brought in the new couch. By the time they removed the old one and placed it in the back of Ian's truck so he could take it to the dump, sweat dripped from his body. Rather than go inside and drench the rugs on the wood flooring when they were finished, he stood on the front porch.

"Would you mind saying goodbye to your father for me?" he asked Daphne after she brought out two bottles of cold water.

"I will," she said before hesitating like there was more but she didn't know how to word it. "He didn't know you were Henry's father. I went to great lengths to hide the fact from him."

Ian opened his, poured half down his throat and the other half over her face and shoulders. Every response that came to mind was stopped by his filter.

"Thank you for your help today, Ian," Daphne said. Her voice still had an effect on him no matter how much he wished it didn't. She'd been his best friend, his first kiss, his first sexual experience...

Ian stopped himself right there before he got all melancholy and lost focus. He shifted his gaze toward Henry's direction. "How should this go down?"

"I have no right to ask this of you, but I was hoping to acclimate him to his new environment before making an official introduction as your father," Daphne said. Hearing those words come out of her mouth still shocked him.

"How long do you plan on sticking around town this time?" he asked, making a dig.

"My dad is sick, Ian. I plan to be here to the end." She hugged her arms across her chest protectively.

"What do you mean he's sick?" he asked, studying her.

"It's a lot to explain now. Another time?" she asked. There was a vulnerability in her voice that stopped Ian from asking a follow-up question.

"And your husband?" he quickly countered. Because it would be too damn tempting to go easy on her when he stared into those cool blue eyes of hers.

"I have an admission to make." She twisted the wedding band on her finger as she shifted her weight from left foot to right.

"There's more?" Ian asked the question more like an accusation. It scored a direct hit.

"Yes, Ian," she started. "I'm not married anymore."

"I noticed," he said.

The look of shock on her face caused him to continue with an explanation.

"When we were moving the chair. I noticed the ring was a little too big and when it moved there was no tan line," he said with a shrug.

"And you didn't want to ask me about it?" she asked, sounding a little defensive.

"Guess I figured you had your reasons," he admitted, figuring she'd gotten a little too comfortable lying.

"Then, why ask about whether or not my husband planned to show up?" she continued.

"I wanted to see how long it would take for you to be honest with me, now that we're face-to-face," he stated.

"Dad doesn't know," she said. "And I'd like to keep it that way for the time being."

He had no idea how she could hide news like that but it wasn't his place to interfere. "What about Henry? Does he think your ex is his father?"

"No," she said quickly.

"Good," he said, but to be honest he wasn't real sure how he felt about any of this news just yet. It would take a minute to process the fact he was father to a nine-year-old and now Mr. Thompson was ill.

"One more thing, Ian," she continued, getting the look she always had when she was having trouble finding the right words. "It wasn't my idea to leave town and keep Henry from you."

"Oh really?" Ian didn't bother to hide the anger in his tone. It wouldn't do any good anyway. There was no covering the raging fire burning through his veins. "Whose was it then?"

"The Marshall's," she said, referring to his grandfather. The man was known to insert himself into other people's business and had done a lot of damage while he'd been alive.

And now those two words would be burned into his heart forever if this was true.

3

"**D**o you want to come in out of the heat?"

Daphne's father poked his head outside and addressed Ian directly. After the bomb she'd just dropped, she couldn't tell if he needed to be as far away from her as possible or if a moving truck couldn't force him off the property.

"Ian's fine, Dad," she said when he didn't immediately respond. She'd just shell-shocked him with the third bomb of the day and it was obvious his mind was reeling as he stood there in silence.

"I'll be inside in a minute, Dad," she continued, hoping —no praying—she hadn't just broken the last bit of good-will left between Ian and her. "Henry probably needs a good shower by now anyway."

"Well, all right," Dad said before thanking Ian for his time and then disappearing. Ian nodded in response but didn't seem able to speak. This was a very bad sign. The longer he stood there mute, the worse this was going to be.

"You said he doesn't know," Ian finally said after a few uncomfortable minutes of silence.

"That's right. He has no idea who Henry belongs to," she said. "I never revealed his father. I disappeared for a while and then resurfaced with a baby. It was hard being away—"

"Hold on right there. I don't want to hear about how hard it was for you when you cut me off and lied to me and everyone close to you," Ian said. The words had a bitter edge to them she probably deserved on some level.

Chin up, she knew it had been the only choice back then.

"First of all, you need to explain to me how the Marshall was involved in your decision to leave town and—"

Ian stopped the second he saw Henry running toward them, with Luis and Luna at his side. His cheeks were fire engine red, and she realized she'd forgotten to put sunblock on him. He'd been out long enough to burn.

"You are covered in dirt, mister," she said as he ran straight to her and wrapped his spindly arms around her midsection. Maybe the coat of dirt would keep his cheeks from peeling. "Shower time and then you can read whatever book you can find."

Ian stood there like a statue. Years ago, she'd learned to give him time and space. He'd always needed time to process big news. Like when he'd been cut from the varsity basketball team in high school. It had taken days for him to process how that could have happened. He'd gone into the head coach and asked him what he could do better. From the next morning on before school, Ian got to the gym early enough to practice his shot. Coach had told Ian that he'd been close to making the team but thought he'd do better on JV another year. By junior year, Ian was starting varsity. He might take time to process but he quickly came up with a game plan when it involved something or someone important to him.

In fact, the summer before senior year when she'd realized her feelings had gone overboard to falling in love, he'd shown up every day at her farmhouse with handpicked flowers to convince her they wouldn't be sacrificing their friendship in order to date. He'd promised to be her friend through thick and thin, even through a breakup if called for.

Henry grumbled as she gave him a hug and a kiss on top of his head. Just yesterday, she held him in her arms as a tiny six-and-a-half-pound baby and now he was shooting up, getting taller every day and making her wish she could find that 'freeze time' button. "Go on. Get cleaned up. It's already supper time and we don't want Pops falling asleep in front of the TV and missing a meal because he had to wait on you."

"I don't know where the bathroom is," Henry complained.

"Pops will show you," she said, confident her dad was having a good enough day to handle the task.

The jaw in Ian's muscle ticked as he watched their interaction. Henry grumbled a little more before giving in and heading inside.

"He's a good kid," Ian managed to say.

"Yes, he is," she agreed.

When no other comments or questions came from Ian, she said, "I'm sure you have questions and you deserve answers. But, right now, I need to go inside and cook. You're welcome to stay. You can ask me anything you want after I finish up dishes and get Henry settled in his room. You deserve that much no matter how awful the Marshall had been to me all those years ago."

Having Ian in the picture complicated things for Daphne. He was the kind of person who would want to swoop in and save the day, thanks to a code of honor too few people shared. If only her situation could be resolved so easily, she would be on that in a heartbeat. This was not only complicated…it was dangerous.

"I just can't, Daphne." With that, Ian turned and walked away. A few seconds later, he was kicking up dust on the drive as he headed toward the farm road and, probably, as far away from her as he could.

Her heart fisted in her chest and all the pain of leaving here without him came crashing down on her, threatening to drag her under and toss her around until she didn't know up from down anymore. She'd done the only thing she could years ago in order to protect Henry. At least, that was what she'd been telling herself for a decade. Seeing Ian now, seeing the hurt and betrayal in his eyes that was put there by her, she wondered if she'd made the right call for Henry, or a selfish one for her.

Daphne fought back hot, angry tears as she tried to stuff down the ball of angry emotions knotting in her throat. She opened the door and then walked inside, trying not to lose it and start crying. She'd imagined the day she would see Ian again. In fact, she'd dreamed about it for the first few years after leaving town. And now, it hurt even more than she'd feared.

"Cowboys are looking good this year," her dad said with a satisfied smile. Her father was positioned in front of the TV with a pre-game on.

"Good for them," she said before making her way to the kitchen and trying her best not fall apart. Her legs could barely hold her weight and part of her wanted to run outside, hop inside the Jeep and beg Ian to come back. What good would it do? Cause him to hate her even more?

She fixed a quick salad and threw a pizza in the oven. By the time Henry came out of the downstairs bedroom with bath attached, plates were on the table. The kid had a sixth sense about pizza. He seemed to know without being told the second a cheese pizza came out of the oven. She located the cutter and used it for cutting slices. Then she threw in an everything pizza for her dad. She landed somewhere in between nothing and everything, but didn't mind picking off the things she didn't like.

"Where'd the man go?" Henry asked, looking around.

"Home, I guess," she said. "The man's name is Ian Firebrand."

Henry shrugged as he took a bite.

"Did you like the man?" she asked, trying to keep the mood light. It wasn't every day a boy met his father without realizing who the man was. Her emotions were all over the place and deep down she really wanted her son to like his father. There was a whole lot of good inside Ian. If Henry was good, it came from his father.

"He was nice," Henry continued. To be nine years old again. So sweet. So innocent. So unaware of the dangers in the world or the fact his life was about to be turned upside-down forever.

"I'm glad you like him," she continued, containing the panic rising in her chest at the thought of sharing Henry with anyone else. It would be the right thing to do, though. Now that Ian was aware of his child, he deserved to have some type of visitation set up. As she remembered, the ranch had security. Part of her wondered if Henry would be safer there while she took care of her ailing father.

The timer dinged. She pulled the second pizza out of the oven and fixed a plate for her dad, who preferred to eat his meals on a TV tray in front of the flatscreen. He looked older sitting there in his lounger. He had more wrinkles. He seemed skinnier. The worst part was that his smile had faded and he'd lost some of that legendary fighting spirit that had him rising before the sun every day to carry on the family legacy. Some of his vitality seemed to have dimmed and she hated the fact he appeared to be giving in.

Emotion clotted in her throat at the thought of her beloved father's condition. She'd already lost most of the last ten years with him. Selfishly, she didn't want to lose him now. Or ever, if wishes were being granted. He'd been the only parent she'd known, considering her mother had left town and never looked back when Daphne was just a little girl, after being caught in an affair.

Her dad had done the best he could with her, she thought as she made her way back to the kitchen and joined Henry at the table. He'd worked his small business and kept food on the table along with a roof over her head. He wasn't an affectionate man, but a day never went by that she didn't feel loved. He'd done fine in her book, and she'd protected him the best way she'd known how.

If only Daphne had known what she would be giving up when she'd agreed to take the deal from the Marshall. Pregnant and scared at eighteen years old, she also hadn't realized she had a choice. Everything was black and white back then and, looking back, she'd been easier to manipulate. The Marshall was gone now and it was probably for the best Henry would never know his great-grandfather. But the devastation and hurt in Ian's eyes earlier would haunt her for the rest of her life.

He would be back. He'd been clear about having a desire to be part of Henry's life. The question was whether or not he hated her enough to bring lawyers with him. A cold shiver raced down her spine at the thought she could lose her son. Ian could only keep Henry away from her until he turned eighteen. Granted, at twelve, he would be able to decide where he lived. Once he found out she'd kept his father from him, would he hate her? Would he resent her for all the moves and never putting down roots?

"What's wrong, Momma?" Henry asked.

She looked over at him only to realize he was studying her.

"Nothing. Why?" she asked a little too quickly.

"Your worry wrinkle is back on your forehead." He pointed to a spot above her eyes.

Daphne forced a smile and rubbed it out. "How about that? Is that better?"

He nodded and smiled before distracting himself with another bite of pizza. If only life could be so easy. Don't like something? Take a bite of pizza. Simple. No one ever got hurt eating pizza.

The thought she could possibly lose Henry caused her heart to fist in her chest. She forced herself to breathe slowly to release some of the tension cording her muscles.

The screen door opened on the back porch. The Dobermans started a low growl as panic gripped Daphne.

"Hey, buddy. I need you to go upstairs now. Run," Daphne instructed, struggling to sound calm. The alarm company wasn't due to come until the morning was her first thought. But she knew they wouldn't be creeping in through the backdoor. An icy chill raced down her back at the thought he might have found her already. Panic squeezed her chest as she glanced around, looking for something...*anything.*

Henry bolted out of the kitchen as a dark male figure moved toward the door, and her. Luna and Luis fired off barks. Hackles raised, snouts aimed directly the back door, the Dobermans locked onto a target as Daphne scanned the countertop for an easy weapon. She reached over and grabbed a knife from the block next to the cutting board on the counter, figuring she could do some damage with the sharp blade. Her hand trembled from stress and adrenaline as her heart threatened to crack through her ribs from hammering so hard.

Just as she raised the knife and positioned herself closer to the door, the figure stopped. He flipped on the porchlight.

The man standing at the backdoor was Ian. Relief flooded her body at the realization. She gave the command for the Dobermans to go find Henry. They retreated as Ian knocked.

THE IMAGE inside the kitchen of a panicked Daphne hoisting a kitchen knife in the air ready to strike was cause for alarm. There were half-full plates on the table and Daphne stood in the middle of the room brandishing a very large, very sharp kitchen knife. Ian tried the door, which had never been locked in all the years he'd been coming here until now.

Daphne replaced the knife inside the block, and then walked over to the door. The snick of the lock came moments before the door opened.

"Did you forget something?" she asked, blocking his entrance. She was a solid foot shorter than him, so he could see right over her head. All those protective instincts from their years together slammed into him at the fear in her eyes. His concern for hers and Henry's safety nearly consumed him. She never would have acted like that if she didn't feel threatened. Since there wasn't much to worry about at her father's place, he assumed she was afraid a threat had followed her home. Didn't that make him want to reach out to her and be her comfort? *Dangerous*, he thought.

"I'd like to come inside and take you up on your offer to talk, if it still stands." He figured this wasn't the right moment to ask about how fast the pulse at the base of her throat thumped. Or the real reason her hands trembled. But questions were racking up.

"Give me a minute," she said, looking like she needed more than one to get her bearings again. She took a step back, enough to allow passage. "You can put on a pot of coffee if you like. Seems like you know where everything is."

The TV was loud enough to cover the conversation going on in the kitchen, so Mr. Thompson probably didn't realize Ian was even there. Since Daphne didn't mention him to her father after she picked up a plate and disappeared, Ian figured she wanted to keep him under wraps.

He fixed a pot of coffee and waited. The machine beeped and still no Daphne. Ian cleaned up the dishes, figuring he could make himself useful. He'd never been good at sitting still while his mind churned on something important. If what Daphne had said about the Marshall was true, Ian had some serious anger to deal with. Considering his grandfather died early in the summer, Ian had no idea where to place his frustration. Until now, he hadn't had any personal reason to hold a grudge but he'd seen the way his grandfather had toyed with his brothers and cousin, and how he'd pitted Ian's father and uncle against each other their entire lives.

The time of giving the man the benefit of the doubt was up. If he was still alive, there would be words.

Since Daphne hadn't returned and he realized her delay most likely had something to do with their son, he went ahead and poured a cup of fresh brew. The creak of footsteps on the wood floor alerted him to her presence before she entered the room.

"Coffee?" he asked without turning around.

"Yes, please." She walked over to the back door and immediately double-checked that she'd locked it. Interesting.

Ian poured her a cup and then met her at the table. He set both mugs down and took the seat her father had been sitting at earlier, watching her with a careful eye. She seemed calmer now and able to breathe again. "You didn't finish your dinner."

"I'm suddenly not very hungry," she said, picking up the coffee instead.

"Does your sudden lack of appetite have anything to do with the fact I'm here?" he asked.

"Truthfully? Yes," she admitted, and he appreciated her honestly. "And because you scared the living daylights out of me surprising me at the backdoor like you did."

"I saw the kitchen light on and figured you'd be back here," he said.

She studied the rim of her coffee cup.

"I have questions," he said before taking a sip.

She nodded, looking like she'd just lost her best friend. That had been him once and he was still scratching his head as to how they'd messed that up.

"You're angry and I get it," she said to him.

"I'd like to talk about what has you so scared first," he said.

"Mind if we *not* go into that right now?" she asked. Something in her voice made him decide to give her a few minutes before circling back to that topic.

"Okay then. Angry is a good word," he agreed.

"I made the best decision I could under the circumstances, which I'm not defending right now," she said. The rim of her cup suddenly became very interesting again.

"We can discuss Henry and how the Marshall fits into the picture in a minute," he said, realizing the threat she was afraid of could be on its way any second. "First, I need to know why the door being locked is so important."

She shook her head.

"Are you trying to tell me the subject is off limits? Because last time I checked, I have a right to know anything and everything that might affect my son," he said with a little more heat than intended.

Daphne's lips compressed into a frown.

"You're right, Ian." She leaned forward, elbows on the table, staring at the rim. "Everything has happened so fast after Dad's diagnosis that I'm still trying to catch my breath and now you're here before I had a chance to figure out the best way to introduce you to Henry."

"Back up for a second." Ian couldn't get past the first thing she said. "You said your father was ill before. What's wrong with your dad?"

"You really don't know?" When she blinked up at him, his heart detonated.

He shook his head.

"Rapid onset dementia," she stated.

A few things Ian had noticed lately clicked into place. For one, Mr. Thompson seemed more forgetful lately. He'd looked downright confused a few times, when Ian showed up after being summoned.

"I'm sorry, Daphne. Your father is a good man and doesn't deserve a diagnosis like that." If anything, his grandfather should have been the one to receive a devastating diagnosis, instead of living to a ripe old age and making everyone miserable in the process. The news he'd been involved in Ian not being told about his son struck like a stray bullet, destruction out of nowhere.

"Thank you, Ian. You don't have to say that, but your kindness means a lot," she said.

"It's for him, not you," he said with a little more ire than intended. What could he say? He was burning up with anger from the inside out and it was difficult to contain.

"Even so," she said, seeming unfazed despite how much his comment must sting. "It's appreciated."

The fact she brought her chin up like she was ready for the next punch made him feel like a real jerk. He wasn't ready to let her off the hook, though. "It's the reason you came home."

"Yes," she said.

"If this hadn't happened," he began, "how long would it have taken before I knew I had a son?"

"That's a fair question," she said, keeping that chin up even though it quivered.

"Dammit, Daphne," he managed to say through clenched teeth. "When did you plan to tell me? When he went to college? Or would you have kept him from me then too?"

"I'm sorry, Ian," she said, not making eye contact.

"It's about nine years too late for that," he quipped. "Or didn't you care what this would do to me when I found out?"

She didn't answer. Instead, she took in a slow, steady breath like she was fortifying herself to take another hit.

"And what about Henry?" he asked. "Didn't he deserve to know his real father?"

The blows kept coming and she sat there and took it. He wanted a fair fight, and this didn't cut it.

"You asked about the lock earlier," she finally said when he stopped talking.

"And the knife in your hand when I caught you off guard. I want to know what that was all about too," he added.

Another sigh came. This one was deep and sounded resigned.

"I think you should take Henry home with you," she said, catching him completely off guard.

"Now?" he asked.

"He's already in bed and we should be okay for one night," she stated as she ran her finger along the cup's rim.

"Daphne, you're not making any sense," he said, needing to understand the about-face. "What kind of trouble are you in?"

4

Daphne didn't even know where to start. There was so much to explain and so little time. She hadn't wanted Ian involved in her messed-up situation, because he would want to fix everything and could end up making it worse. Although, it was hard to imagine how any of this could get worse right now.

"Promise me you'll take Henry and keep him safe. Then I'll explain," she said.

"You're not in a position to make demands, Daphne," he pointed out. There was a mix of shock and frustration in his eyes, a storm brewed.

"No, I'm not," she admitted. "But it's not safe here for Henry. The minute word gets out that I'm home, trouble will follow."

"Why is that and what kind?" His forehead creased with deep concern lines.

"It's my mess, Ian. I need to clean it up. It's time anyway," she said, exhaling and feeling like she was finally letting out a breath she'd been holding for two long years. "I got myself into a relationship that went sour. My ex got involved in a crime ring with his cousin. His gang seemed to think I betrayed him by walking out even though the relationship soured and he wasn't good to me."

"Why on earth would you get involved with someone like that?" Ian's disgust was a knife stab to the chest.

"Because he wasn't like that when we first met," she defended. "He was good to Henry."

"What changed?" Ian asked as the muscles in his face tensed.

"The band he was in broke up and he spiraled after that," she said. "I met him when things were good and he was on a high. He asked me to marry him and I said yes. Henry was four years old and I think part of me wanted to give him the one thing that was missing, his father."

She glanced over at Ian in time to see him white-knuckle the coffee mug. Hearing this now as the words came out of her mouth made her sad and she could only imagine the impact they were having on Ian.

"I was young and stupid. I didn't think I'd ever be allowed to see you again. My heart was broken and it never recovered," she explained.

"You didn't think to call me and explain what was happening at one time?" he finally said. There was so much bitterness in his tone she tensed up.

"I thought about it *all* the time, *every* minute of the day, but I also realized I was no match for the Marshall," she admitted. Hearing those words come out after holding them inside for so long caused some of the heavy blanket that had been wrapped around her shoulders to lift.

"You mentioned him before. What could he have possibly done?" Ian asked as the storm intensified behind his eyes. With every word, every explanation, she seemed to only be hurting him worse. Her heart was practically bleeding for how awful she felt in this moment and the worst part was that there was nothing she could do or say to make it better for Ian. The anger brewing behind his brown eyes startled her. In all their years of friendship, she'd never seen anything close to this.

"He found out that I was pregnant before I had a chance to tell you. He paid me a visit and threatened me. Said I would ruin your future if I told you, and that meant he had the right to ruin mine. He threatened to make certain I would never lay eyes on my child once it was born and that he would tie me up in court so long my kid would be grown before I would meet it." The admission stung even now and it felt like her breath was knocked out of her, even knowing logically the man was gone and couldn't hurt her or Henry any longer. It was almost like he still had the power to reach out from the grave and hurt her and her son. She involuntarily shivered at the memory. For a long time after their meeting, she saw his face when she closed her eyes at night.

"That's all it took to get you to leave me and withhold my child from me all these years? An idle threat?" the disappointment in his tone was another physical blow. She deserved it and more.

"It sure didn't feel idle to an eighteen-year-old kid," she stated in her defense. "When I told him that you had a right to know and refused to leave town, he threatened my father and his business." The painful memory brought up all the sadness and hurt from a decade ago. Pain it had taken years to learn to live with and she still wasn't certain she'd succeeded.

"Why would he do that?" Ian asked, sounding a little dumbfounded.

"You don't know?" she asked. "Really, Ian?"

"What's that supposed to mean?" The defensiveness in his tone caught her off guard.

"The richest man in town is used to getting what he wants, for starters," she said. "Your grandfather made it known to me that he didn't think I was good enough for you."

"That's insane," Ian defended. "Why would he even care?"

She shot him a look that sent hot daggers toward him.

Ian held up a hand to stop her from continuing. "Never mind. Don't answer that. I didn't know the man very well personally. I always kept a distance from him and my father, if I'm honest, but with everything I've been hearing since the beginning of summer, I probably shouldn't be shocked." He paused long enough to take a sip of coffee like he needed a minute to slow down and absorb. He'd always been like that and it was comforting to realize not everything had changed.

"What's been happening?" she quickly asked, wondering how safe it was to bring Henry here.

"A whole lot," he said. "Nothing I want to get into right now, though."

She relented with a nod before taking a sip of coffee.

"We used to tell each other everything, Daphne."

She nodded.

"You should have come to me," he said, his voice a little calmer now. "I would have worked it out."

He'd been eighteen years old and had never gone against his family in his life. Her father's livelihood had been threatened.

"It was an impossible situation, Ian," she said quietly. "But I doubt you'll ever see it that way."

He didn't respond and that wasn't a good sign.

"You never answered my question," she stated, figuring she'd said enough for one night. She didn't have a whole lot of time to come up with a game plan on how to handle her ex, Miles Nolan, and his cousin when they arrived. And she had a feeling they *would* make an appearance.

Ian's eyebrow shot up. "About what?"

"Taking Henry to live with you for a little while," she hedged.

"Wouldn't that be hard on him?" he asked. "I mean, you're the only parent he's ever known. Suddenly, he's in a new place with different surroundings." He waved his hand around to make a point about moving to her father's. "If I take him home with me, won't that confuse him?"

"If anything happened to him..." A sob escaped before she could reel it back in.

"This ex of yours," Ian said, his voice a low rumble. "Tell me more about him."

"Suffice it to say he isn't the type to take it well when someone divorces him," she said. "Even though it was two years ago, he has a long memory."

"Where have you and Henry been living since the divorce?" Ian asked.

Daphne stared Ian in the eyes for a long moment. What she was about to admit was the hardest thing since walking out on Miles. "At first, in a battered women's shelter."

"He put his hands on you?" Ian was suddenly on his feet, pacing the small kitchen.

"Once, but mostly he just threatened to hurt me or threatened to hurt Henry to get to me," she said on a shrug as though she could shake off the hurt from that time in her life. Easier just to tell the story as if it had happened to someone else. Try not to remember. Try not to relive...

"Emotional abuse is just as serious as physical," Ian said sharply. A man with his moral code would take neither lightly.

"I couldn't agree more," she said, then added, "I was really young and naïve. Looking back, there were so many signs the relationship would be unstable, but I didn't see any of them coming." She could feel her cheeks heat from embarrassment. It was so hard to admit her past mistakes to someone who had always been so perfect.

"Being tricked into thinking someone is different than they really are doesn't make you foolish," Ian countered as he walked straight over to her. He lifted her chin up until their eyes met. "It makes you human and vulnerable."

"Which allows other people to take advantage of you," she added. Never again would she fall into that trap. After Miles, she'd sworn off relationships. The only men she needed in her life were her father and Henry. And now it looked like Henry's father would be there too. Processing the turn of events in the past week would take serious doing. There was so much to unpack. Because his hand on her chin while she stared into the depths of those intense brown eyes made her want nothing more than to stand up and kiss him, which would lead to nothing but disaster.

"RATHER THAN TAKE Henry with me and pull him away from the only people he knows, how about I stay here instead?" Ian had no qualms about putting her ex and his cousin in their place if they showed up on her family's land.

"I don't know, Ian." Daphne shook her head and her unease about the subject was palpable. "It's risky and I would be putting you in danger as well."

"Don't worry about me," he quickly countered, hoping he could convince her. The more he thought about it, the better he liked the idea. "It would give me a chance to get to know Henry in a non-threatening environment. You wouldn't have to worry about him." He motioned toward the other room. "You already have two serious guard dogs. I'm guessing that was on purpose on your part."

"They're trained to protect Henry," she said, nodding.

Ian wasn't quite ready to forgive her but he also realized lingering in the past would only hurt the here and now, and damage the future. If he didn't handle his relationship with Henry right, the kid might never want to come to the ranch.

"Someone needs to protect you," he said, looking her straight in the eye. "I'd like it to be me."

Her mouth twisted in the way it always did when she was about to protest something he said or was about to do.

"Hear me out." He put a hand up to stop her, hoping to get her agreement. If they were going to co-parent, and he hoped they would, both needed to learn to cooperate. Just because they didn't love each other like they had in the past, didn't mean they couldn't get their relationship on solid footing.

She gave a slight nod as she picked up her coffee cup with both hands. Rolling the cup with her palms, she lifted an eyebrow. "Go ahead, but I have to say that—"

"No 'buts' until you hear what I have to say," he countered, hoping she would keep an open mind.

Again, she nodded.

"Henry needs to be comfortable if I'm going to make ground with him. I'd like to see him in as normal an environment as possible. If you're the only constant he's had in his life, I don't want to take that away. Even for a minute," he began.

"Does that mean you won't take him away from me through the courts?" she asked.

"Is that a serious question? That one hurts, Daphne." In order to calm his flaring temper, he stalked to the kitchen door, unlocked it, and walked outside into the night air. It was early enough in September for the temperatures to remain in the high eighties to nineties even at this time of night. The familiar chirps of cicadas and wide open night sky, with stars that seemed to go on for days, calmed his nerves. Getting angry with Daphne wouldn't get him very far and pretty much everything about this situation caused his temper to flare, beginning with the fact she'd withheld his child from him for nearly a decade. Don't even get him started on her ex. The man sounded like a class-A bastard. Ian's hands fisted thinking about the man she'd married when it should have been him. Times had changed. He'd changed. Staying calm when his world had been turned upside down required fresh air and a few calming breaths.

Hands on his hips, he scanned the area. The yard was good sized but there was a tree line that anyone could exploit. Binoculars. A long-range rifle. He canceled the second thought. This crime was personal. Her ex and his cousin would want to be up close to watch the life drain out of her. Revenge killings generally involved being strangled or stabbed.

Ian issued a sharp sigh. There was no way he was leaving tonight with those images stamped in his thoughts. He also realized how desperate she must be to ask him, a virtual stranger now despite their history, to take Henry and keep him safe. It also showed that, deep down, she still had a whole lot of trust in Ian. He might be the only person in the world she would trust with her son under the circumstances. He reminded himself to stay focused on the positives and not get carried away with thinking about her betrayal. Easier said than done considering the circumstances.

Calmer, he walked back inside the house.

"I can take Henry with me," he said to her. "But I won't sleep knowing you're here vulnerable. He'll be in a new environment with a stranger and I don't think that's the best situation for him either."

Daphne hung her head low. "You're right. I know that. I'm desperate here, Ian. I can't take my father away from the only home he's ever known—especially with his diagnosis —and, on some level, I realize that I can't keep moving every few months when I see someone who looks like Miles. At some point he's going to see me first. I can't stay on the run." She blew out a breath and he could have sworn he saw her chest deflate. "Henry should be in school and have friends other than his dogs. Although, he loves them dearly."

"I'm certain he does," Ian reassured.

"This is no way for him to live, Ian. Even I know that," she said, sounding defeated. The spunky attitude that he'd always loved about her had momentarily gone.

Setting his anger aside, he realized the best way to get her to agree to let him stay was to show her that he still cared what happened to her.

"He seems like a great kid, Daphne. You've done right by him." Ian probably shouldn't want to comfort her and yet he couldn't deny how right it was to be back in this kitchen, the two of them together with her father in the next room.

"Henry is amazing despite my parenting skills," she said, putting her head in her hands.

The temptation to pull her to standing and hold her was a physical ache. Muscle memory, he decided. He'd loved

Daphne for a long time. That love was burned into every fiber of his being. Seeing her again dredged up old feelings and nothing more, he told himself.

But why was he trying so hard to convince himself of that?

5

The TV turned off in the next room. The sound of her father's shoes shuffling across the wood floor echoed in the house. Daphne made tentative eye contact with Ian as her father yelled, "You kids be good in there."

Ian's face broke into a smile despite the tension between them, filling the room. The break was nice.

"To be kids again," she said wistfully, as she picked up the cup of coffee and drained the contents.

Ian laughed and the sound sent her pulse racing. This wasn't the time or place to let her feelings take the wheel. Besides, how could she not feel something when the father of her child was in the same room—a room they'd been in countless times before and held so many good memories between them.

Daphne cleared her throat in a lame attempt to refocus. "I have an alarm company coming to install a system in the morning."

"Good," Ian stated, back to his all-business tone. It was for the best this way. Neither needed to get caught up in nostalgia and lose sight of the reason they were here... protect Henry at all costs. "What else?"

"I sleep with a loaded shotgun underneath my mattress, and a stun gun under my pillow strong enough to give the recipient a perm he won't soon forget," she stated with a little more authority. There were times when her nerves got the best of her, and she didn't think she could keep going. Those were instances when she reminded herself how much of a kick-butt person she truly was.

"Even better," Ian said with a smirk. He would get a kick out of the fact she slept with a military-grade stun gun within reach every time she closed her eyes. "Are you unpacked yet?"

"Not really. I pulled out Henry's sheets and his favorite blanket to give him some sense of normalcy," she said. "He handles it all well, but the moves have to stop. He's getting older and he needs me to put down roots."

"You don't have to convince me," Ian stated.

She had said those words a little loudly and with purpose. It had been her mantra for the past twenty-four months and she was determined to make it happen one way or another. Even if it meant introducing Henry to his father and then turning her son over while she sorted out her personal life and took care of her father.

"Thank you for volunteering to stay over," she said, realizing she'd forgotten to thank him earlier. He'd showered and had that fresh citrusy scent that she'd always loved. The kitchen was so small all she could do was breathe him in. She got hit with a bout of nostalgia that threatened to tug her under, drown her in memories.

"You're welcome," he said before reclaiming his seat and then leaning over the table. He took her hands in his and all kinds of electrical impulses lit up her body. Impulses she needed to get in check before he could see her body's reaction to him. "You don't have to do this alone anymore, Daphne."

Those words were a life raft in the raging storm that had become her life for too long.

"We don't have to have everything figured out on day one," he continued. His words soothed her, heart and soul. "This is a work-in-progress."

"You have no idea how much it means to have you in my corner," she said, feeling the roughness of his fingers against her skin.

Ian pulled his hands back and she felt the cold immediately. He said, "I'm in Henry's corner and always will be. You can count on me being here for anything he needs. I want to get to know my son and be involved in his life. We need to talk about what his financial needs are and will be, and what visitation might look like."

A wall came up between them. She needed to remind herself every day Ian was here because of his son and his help had nothing to do with any love he might have felt for her. Their relationship was ancient history. She was thankful for the reminder before she went too far down the road of thinking he still cared about her.

"Honestly, I just want to get through today." She stood up and double-checked the lock on the backdoor.

"I'll sleep in Henry's room tonight. You can take my old bed upstairs. Word of warning, though, it probably still has the same purple silk sheets on it from ten years ago," she said, feeling the chill between them now. "I'll check the front door as I head upstairs. You can stay up as long as you like. I don't have to tell you where anything is, since you've probably been here more times than me in the past decade."

Ian stood up and put his hands on his hips looking like he wasn't sure why the air in the room had just changed.

It was for the best this way, she reminded herself. She would add those words to her daily mantra too, if it helped her remember.

IAN'S MIND RACED. Since he never knew when he might need an overnight trip to track poachers on the ranch, he always kept a bag with supplies in his truck. Before he stepped outside, he figured he needed to let Daphne know. She seemed determined to keep the doors locked and he would lose visual with the front door for thirty seconds or so while he grabbed the bag inside his truck. Henry's room was the downstairs guestroom. Ian crossed the living room and then lightly tapped on the bedroom door.

Daphne cracked it. The lights were dimmed behind her.

"He sleeps with a nightlight," she whispered, by way of explanation.

Ian's heart sank when he saw that she was trying to cover up the fact she'd been crying. "Everything okay?"

"Me? Yes," she said with a sniffle. "Hold on. Let me come out there."

He retreated into the living room, figuring he might be the biggest jerk on earth. She was shaken up after their conversation in the kitchen. She'd gone cold when he'd mentioned the fact he wanted to be here for his son. Was that the problem? Did she feel rejected by him? A growing part of him wanted to be here for Daphne too. But the other part that remembered how much she'd shattered him kept him from it. At this point, the only thing he could commit to was seeing her through the current threat. *One day at a time*, he reminded.

Daphne stepped inside the room.

"I was about to grab an overnight bag from my truck, but realized you might get scared if you didn't know what was happening," he explained.

"That's thoughtful of you, Ian." Her tone was all business and lost some of the softness from the kitchen. At least the fear was gone as well.

"You can keep an eye on the door while I pop outside," he said.

She crossed her arms over her chest. "Good idea."

"I'll be right back," he said and then waited for her to nod.

She did, so he unlocked the front door and headed outside. Grabbing his bag took less than thirty seconds and she stood sentinel at the door waiting for his return, watching. This ex of hers had her worried. She'd mentioned spending the past two years on the run. He tightened his grip on the handle of the bag and tried not to give into the anger boiling the blood in his veins.

At least she was here now where he could protect her. Ian had no plans to leave Daphne to her own devices. She was the mother of his child and someone important. Henry needed his mother around. Period. And not have her constantly looking over her shoulder.

Ideas were forming as to the kind of help he could offer and he wanted to speak to her first thing in the morning about it. For tonight, enough had been said between them.

"Do you have a pen and piece of paper I could borrow, before you head for bed?" he asked.

"I think they are still in the same place. Hold on a second," she said after relocking the door behind him. She cut across the room and to the built-in desk in the corner. After opening a couple of drawers, she held up a yellow memo pad. Then, pens from another drawer.

"Are these good enough?" she asked, holding up the offerings.

He nodded.

"They probably still work, although they may have been inside here for the past decade," she said with a small smile.

"I know where to look now if these are defective," he said, thinking he needed to map out a safety plan first and then he could put some thought into a financial arrangement. Ian was beginning to process the reality he was a father, and ideas were starting to percolate.

"Goodnight, Ian," Daphne said as she suppressed a yawn.

"Night," he said to her, figuring he could pour another cup of coffee before heading upstairs. Granted, he remembered how to access her bedroom window better from outside.

A thought struck. Having her and Henry on the ground floor wasn't the safest. He could set up at the kitchen table, or even on the sofa.

The table won out after a quick debate. He could see the front and back door from there. Leaving the light on might deter someone from making a move. He went around pulling the blinds down to make anyone inside the house less of a target. It was impossible to shoot what someone couldn't see clearly.

Since Ian hadn't had a chance to make friends with Henry's dogs, it was probably for the best they were inside the bedroom with him and Daphne.

After refilling his mug, he took a seat at the table in the eat-in kitchen. The table was at the center of the room, so it should be safe as long as he stayed away from windows. A shadow could give away his location.

First things first, he needed to attend to the safety plan. There were plenty of items that could easily be installed around the outside of the house to alert him if someone was trying to make a nighttime approach. Ian briefly thought about bringing his brothers in to take shifts and keep watch outside, but he needed to dig up a little more research on what Daphne's ex was capable of before he sounded any alarms.

Then, there was Henry to consider. His introduction to the Firebrand family was important and Ian wanted to make sure Daphne led the charge. She had been bringing up Henry on her own for the past nine and a half years and seemed to be doing a standup job. Despite still dealing with his anger about how he found out about Henry and the fact his son had been kept from him, Ian wanted to co-parent with Daphne. He wanted his son to see his parents getting along and working together in his best interest.

Ian paused for a few seconds to digest this revelation. This wasn't how he saw himself becoming a father. To be fair, Ian hadn't seen himself becoming a father at all, so this was a real shocker. He could let himself get caught up in the fact nine and a half years of his son's life had been stolen from him and from Henry. Or Ian could decide to let the past stay as water under the bridge and move on. Since he couldn't go back and change a thing, he decided moving on was for the best. He couldn't begin to imagine how stressful it must have been for Daphne to have the wealthiest man in town and one of the richest in all of Texas threatening her and her father. The Marshall knew how to hit deep, Ian was learning. His respect for the man was at an all-time low. Ian couldn't confront him either. All the anger building inside him would have to be dealt with another way.

He tapped the pen on the pad of paper before writing down motion-sensing lights. Those would be easy enough to install. Daphne had arrived today, so they might have a day or two depending on how quick her ex was and how badly he wanted to find her.

Cameras were the second thing he jotted down. There were all kinds of DIY systems nowadays. Anyone with a computer and a screwdriver could set up a decent system. Between those two things and the alarm that would be installed come morning, Ian figured they would be in good shape by late afternoon. He texted his list to Bronc Harris, longtime ranch foreman, and asked him if he could have someone bring those items by in the morning before nine a.m. That would give Ian plenty of daylight to get everything installed. He could work alongside the alarm system installer to give Daphne some peace.

Ian rolled the sheet of paper up and over, moving onto the second sheet. He marked the header as, *finances*. This would be somewhat easy. He could contact Manny Ortega, the family accountant, to set up a trust for Henry and an allowance that would give Daphne the option of working or not until Henry turned eighteen. Call Ian a renaissance man, but he believed a mother should have the right to stay home with a child, if family finances could spare it and if she wanted to do so. Speaking of which, he needed to ask Daphne what she'd done for money over the past two years. She had to have been doing something to bring enough cash in to pay the bills.

Then there was the issue of Henry's schooling to think about. There were plenty of homeschooled or virtually schooled kids these days, so she might have him in one of those programs. Daphne seemed upset Henry had spent so much time alone in the past two years. Something needed to be done about it. If Ian had to escort the kid himself, he'd do it.

Ian bit back a curse at the thought she'd had to be on the run in the first place not to mention afraid of the one person who should vow to protect them. No person should have to be scared of their partner, married or otherwise. He realized his grip on the pen had tightened considerably because this wasn't just any person. This was Daphne. The woman he'd once believed he would spend the rest of his life loving and protecting until the Marshall had interfered. More of that anger surfaced. Ian took a couple of deep breaths.

Another thought struck, he was already starting to imagine him and Henry on fishing trips together. The kid seemed to like being outside. They had something in common there. Something they could build on?

There was a whole lot more to do and he wondered how readily Daphne would take money from him. She had an independent streak a mile long and from the looks of it, not much had changed in that department. Was there a way to set her up with the money without offending her or making her feel like a charity case? From what he'd seen of his brother Adam's child, these kiddos were more than a full-time job. She deserved back pay for the past nine and a half years. Could he take that angle?

His laptop was at home. He rarely ever kept it with him and didn't think he'd need it when he got the call from Mr. Thompson. There wasn't much he could do tonight other than make plans.

The bedroom door opened and Henry walked out. Daphne must still be asleep or she would no doubt trail behind the kiddo. Ian checked the time and a surprising two hours had passed.

"My throat hurts," Henry said. He stood there with a brown teddy bear dangling from his hand. His hair was tousled and he had on button down pajamas with horses and various farm animals stamped on them. The kid was adorable and seeing him look so small and sleepy nearly ripped Ian's heart out of his chest.

"Do you want a drink of water?" Ian was at a loss as to what to do.

Henry nodded as he brought his free hand up to his throat. Even in this light, his cheeks were red. Ian had been around his brother Adam and his kid enough to realize that wasn't a good thing.

Ian stood up, unsure exactly what to do next though. His first thought was to wake Daphne but she'd looked tired earlier and in need of rest. Moving days were exhausting and she'd been under more stress than any person should have to be. He might not agree with the decisions she'd made but he could concede the Marshall could be convincing when he needed to be and threatening too. The fallout from his deeds was still raining down on the Firebrand family and the results weren't good.

"Why don't you sit down on the couch and I'll get a glass of water?" Ian said to Henry.

Henry walked over and plopped down. His shoulders were hunkered forward and there was none of the earlier excitement or energy in his eyes. As Ian tried to leave the room, he heard a low growl coming from the darkened doorway of the bedroom. There would be no flying under the radar on this one.

One of the large Dobermans came out, followed by the second. Since there would be no getting close to Henry without waking Daphne, Ian conceded and made a large circle around the living room on his way to wake her.

"I'm going to wake your mother so the dogs don't decide to take a bite out of me," he explained to Henry. "And then we'll get your water."

"Okay," Henry's voice was small and frail-sounding. All of Ian's protective instincts flared and he knew in an instant he would give his life for this kid if it came down to it. Becoming a father was a force beyond anything Ian had ever experienced.

"Daphne," Ian whispered as he entered the guestroom. The nightlight kept him from tripping over the suitcase that had been placed on the floor at the foot of the bed. He moved beside her and took a knee. Seeing her sleeping so peacefully gave him second thoughts about waking her and yet she would want to know what was happening with Henry. Ian also needed her help with the Dobermans. And yet, seeing her lying there with her blonde locks spilled out over the pillow caused his heart to squeeze. For just a moment, he was taken back to all those times he'd sneaked inside her room at night so he could hold her while she fell asleep. His fingers itched to reach out and touch her again. The low growl at the door stopped him.

"Hey," he said a little louder this time. When she didn't respond, he gently shook her.

Daphne bolted upright and pulled her covers up to her neck as she scooted away from him in what looked like a state of panic.

"It's me, Daphne. Ian Firebrand," he reassured, taken back by the sudden movement and the fear in her eyes.

She blinked a couple of times as she brought her hand up and removed a long strand of hair from her lips—lips he had no business looking at or wanting to kiss until she wasn't afraid any longer.

"Ian?" She looked around like she was trying to get her bearings. And then she seemed to realize her son wasn't next to her. "Where's Henry?"

6

"Henry's cheeks look like he's burning with fever. The Dobermans don't want me getting close to him. I need your help."

Daphne's pulse raced. Her heart felt like it might explode out of her ribcage as she heard the news. "Where is he?"

"In the living room," Ian said. "I wanted to handle it myself but the dogs came out growling, and I wasn't in the mood to pick Doberman teeth out of my backside."

"Oh. Sorry. They just have to get used to you." She wasted no time throwing her covers off and racing into the next room. Henry sat on the sofa like all the energy had been drained from his body. She felt his forehead. "Baby, you're burning up. Let Mommy get you something for your fever."

"What can I do?" Ian sounded helpless and that wasn't something she ever thought she'd hear in a Firebrand's voice.

"Do you mind getting a glass of water and finding ibuprofen? I probably have some packed somewhere but I think my dad should have some in the cabinet. Check the date, though," she stated, hoping the pill bottle would be more recently bought than the yellow pad of paper.

Ian disappeared into the kitchen and then she heard cabinets being opened and closed as she reassured Henry.

"Let's get you back to bed, okay?" she said to her son.

Henry nodded, looking like he might burst into tears at any moment.

"Want me to carry you?" she asked.

Again, he nodded.

Daphne picked him up and he wrapped his little arms around her neck. Little? The joke was on her, because he was getting so tall that his feet practically dragged the floor as she struggled to bring him back to bed. She placed him on his side as Ian came rushing into the room.

"Can he take Advil?" he asked.

"One," she stated, thinking she didn't have a pediatrician here in Lone Star Pass yet, and how that might affect her son's health. It pretty much made her feel like the worst mother on the planet.

Ian handed over the coated pill and glass of water. She helped Henry sit up enough to swallow the pill and wash it down. She propped pillows up so he could lie back until the medicine worked its magic.

Next, she told the dogs to back down. Luna settled first and then Luis finally joined her. Both stayed on high alert.

"See if you can sleep. Okay, buddy?" she soothed.

"My head hurts too," Henry complained.

"I know," she said. If this was strep, he would need an antibiotic. They'd only been at the last pediatrician for two months and Henry had always been a healthy kid. Would it be strange if she called the office out of the blue?

Glancing over at Ian, there was just enough light to outline the panic on his face. "What else can I do?"

"Would you mind bringing a cool, wet hand towel over, for his forehead?" she asked, figuring it would help Henry until the medicine kicked in and give something Ian to do in the meantime.

Ian was on it. He disappeared out of the room faster than she could blink. The same worried expression scored his face that she probably had the first time Henry had been sick as an infant. She'd been tempted to drive straight back to the hospital where he'd been born two weeks earlier and beg for help. A sweet neighbor overheard his crying and knocked on the door to check on mother and baby. The woman became like a grandmother to Henry and had been a godsend to Daphne. Nina Eli had been a gift from the heavens. The older woman had kept mostly to herself, since the neighborhood in Austin wasn't 'the greatest' as she'd put it. Ms. Nina said the two of them moving next door breathed in new life to the apartment complex. At eighty-six, she'd been one of the wisest people Daphne had ever known. Her help in getting Daphne through those first few weeks and months had been more than Daphne figured she ever deserved after the way she'd been forced to leave things with Ian.

Mother and baby had survived those early medical scares. Ms. Nina had made it to her ninetieth birthday, just as she'd hoped and Daphne missed the sweet woman to this day. Looking back, it wasn't long after that Miles had come into Daphne's life.

She had been in mourning. Had feeling that she'd lost everything important to her again left her vulnerable? In hindsight, the answer was a resounding *yes*. Too bad she couldn't see it at the time. But then, Miles had been on top of his game. He'd been charming...a little too much so? Most of all, he'd been good to Henry.

Ian returned, breaking into her melancholy thoughts with relief for Henry in Ian's hands.

She looked up at him and mouthed a *thank you*. He nodded as she turned to place the cool towel on Henry's forehead. The sore throat troubled her because that was an almost sure sign of strep.

Ian pulled out his cell phone. "I can have our family doctor here in..." he checked his watch. "Less than an hour."

"You have a family doctor on call twenty-four-seven?" Daphne held a hand up as soon as the words left her mouth. "Of course you do. You're a Firebrand. It's easy to forget how rich you really are when you're so darn down to earth."

Ian was already preoccupied with the call before she'd finished her sentence. Why go to the hospital when a doctor will come to you? The thought made her want to laugh which only reminded her how slap-happy she'd become. Lack of sleep didn't do good things to the brain.

"Dr. Ynez is on his way," Ian said before stabbing his fingers through his thick mane. He caught Daphne's gaze. She must have shot him a look because he quickly added, "What?"

She shook her head. "Nothing, Ian. I'm grateful to have a doctor on the way after a snap of your fingers, but it's just not something I'm used to. Stuff like this doesn't happen to people in the real world, so it'll take some getting used to. Henry will have to get used to it too."

Their tiny world was changing and it scared her. Once her son got to know his father and saw the amazing ranch he could live on, would he even want to be around her again? Or would he gravitate toward Ian and the next thing she knew, she'd be cut out of his life by his own choosing?

"You've done an amazing job with him, Daphne," Ian said, cutting into her heavy thoughts. She wasn't feeling sorry for herself, just being practical. If she had the choice between living on the Firebrand family's ranch or being with her, she'd probably take the ranch too.

"He loves animals," she said quietly.

Ian seemed to pick up on her line of thinking. "Hey, I'm sorry if I overstepped my bounds here. I have a tendency to act first and think later. Usually, my instincts are spot-on, and I've gotten used to trusting them without giving anything else a second thought. But this is something else so—"

"I'll stop you right there. This is a good thing, Ian. I'm grateful to have a doctor at your disposal to be able to make sure Henry is going to be fine," she stated. "It's just a huge change from checking the calculator app on my phone to make sure I have enough cash at the grocery store to having a doctor practically on call for all Henry's personal needs."

"Yours too," Ian interjected, before realizing he might not be making this easier. "Again, I apologize. But I look at it this way, Henry needs his mother to be healthy and in tip-top shape. You can't do that if you don't have access to the best medical care."

When he put it like that, it sounded well thought-out and reasonable. As long as the financial train stopped there.

She turned her attention toward her son, pressing her palm to his forehead after removing the now-warm towel. "His temp is going down."

Henry's eyes stayed closed and his breathing became steady. The medicine was doing its job. Daphne sighed in relief.

"Why don't you lie down beside him while I go out front and wait for the doc?" Ian asked.

"Actually, would you stay here for a second while I run to the restroom and grab a drink of water for myself?" She didn't want to drink after her son and take a risk of catching whatever he had. Strep was only one possibility. Others could be transmitted to her and the last thing she needed or wanted was to go down sick today. Besides, she was here to take care of her father, not the other way around, despite how much Ian made her think life might have taken a turn for the better.

Dangerous thought.

"Absolutely. Go," Ian said without hesitation.

She thanked him before heading down the hallway to the bathroom and then toward the kitchen. As she cut through the living room, she glanced down at the yellow memo pad. Right there, in big letters, Ian had outlined what else he'd be doing for her and Henry.

Daphne sat down on the living room carpet and grabbed hold of the paper. She blinked at the large sum of money that would be put in trust for Henry. Apparently, she wasn't supposed to work either. There was an amount that 'should' get her through to Henry's eighteenth birthday. Then what was she supposed to do with her life? Did Ian think about that? Or did he care about what she thought *she* wanted to do with her life?

Granted, she was still young and Henry would be of age in eight and a half years, but still. She had plans that didn't include handing over the reins to Ian Firebrand so he could tell her what and when to do. Her body involuntarily shuttered at the memory of the Marshall poking his finger in her chest, telling her to get out of town before he drove her and her father out.

Rather than sit here and get too worked up about the paper, she dropped it onto the coffee table and pushed up to standing. This wasn't the time or place for the argument that was coming. Right now, the only thing that mattered was getting Henry healthy again. In the meantime, she would try to shake off the horrible memory of Marshall Firebrand.

Daphne issued a sharp sigh. What was it about a Firebrand that made them believe they could push her around? She'd listened to the Marshall and this was where she ended up. A voice in the back of her head reminded her that she wasn't young and naïve any longer. A grown woman made her own decisions and took charge of her own life. Now that she'd left Dallas when her second year at community college was just getting started, she would have to regroup and find a new program. She had no intention of walking away from her degree in Arts and Technology. She'd already worked it out in her mind that being able to work from home as a web designer would be the best course of action for her and Henry until he went to college. And she could accomplish it without a Firebrand giving her the blessing.

IAN HAD NEVER FELT SO helpless in his entire life. Standing beside his son's bed while the kid had burned with fever had to have been the most miserable feeling in the world. He would take that kid's sickness if it would make Henry better. Thankfully, Daphne had known exactly what to do. The doc would be here soon, and they would have answers about what had made Henry so sick in the first place.

One of the Dobermans made a low, throaty growl as Ian crossed over toward the bed. He was good with animals if given enough time and would win over the two who'd been protecting his son. The growls didn't upset Ian. They said the dogs were doing their job. But he also didn't want to get bitten, so he moved back toward the door.

Daphne returned, so he stepped aside to allow passage.

"They sure are fond of Henry," he said as he motioned toward the animals.

"Is that why you're here, instead of sitting at the foot of the bed?" she asked. Something had changed in her voice since leaving the room.

"Maybe," he said. "Hey, can we step out into the hallway?"

He'd learned watching his family fights while growing up that it was never good to let anything fester.

Daphne followed him, stopping at the door and crossing her arms over her chest—a chest he didn't need to distract himself by looking at.

"What's wrong?" he asked.

She shot him a confused look but he knew different.

"Come on," he whispered. "You walked out of here fine and came back irritated. Why?"

"Fine." She dropped her gaze. "I saw the memo pad in the living room, Ian. I didn't ask for your help and we don't need it."

"Is this about the money?" he asked, doing his best to hide his frustration at her refusal of his help.

"Yes and no," she said.

"Well, that answer is about as clear as a bell," he whispered with a little more heat than intended.

"Money is great. For you. Henry and I live modestly, and we've been getting along fine," she explained. "I don't see why he needs a trust fund."

"He's a Firebrand," Ian countered. "It comes with the last name."

"No offense, but all I've seen money do is drive a wedge between your family." She brought a hand to her mouth like she regretted those words the second they came out.

"I won't deny money can cause problems when people allow it to," he said. It was true. He'd seen how greed had motivated his grandfather, father, and uncle. The three of them could have been close but the Marshall pitted the two against each other. They'd recently found out there'd been other reasons for the Marshall's ways but none that excused his behavior in Ian's book. Explained maybe, but not excused.

"And what would be different about us?" she asked, placing her hand on her hip. "You've barely known Henry a day and you're already making out lists of what you're going to give him and do for me. What about my plans?"

"I just wanted to help," he argued. He could be stubborn when he wanted to be. She knew him better than most and would realize that he could dig his heels in when he wanted to.

"Remember that time business had been slow all summer, and I packed my lunch at the start of school? Out of nowhere, I get a note from the office saying they found money left in my lunch account from the previous year," she pressed.

Ian's jaw dropped open, but he didn't speak. He'd had no idea she figured him out.

"You might want to close that," she said, motioning toward his lips. "I asked you if you were responsible and told you to take the money back."

"I was honest with you about it. *I* didn't. The money belonged to my family and what's the point of having it if I couldn't—if I can't—do something good to help a friend," he explained.

"But I didn't *want* your charity, Ian," she rebutted. "I didn't want to *owe* you anything. You or anyone else, but especially you. We were best friends who were on equal footing, and you paying for things stripped that away."

"That wasn't how I saw things, Daphne. I still don't," he said.

"What did you do when I tried to return the money?" she asked.

Again, he didn't respond.

"Uh-huh. I thought so," she stated. "We both know my dad's layaway suddenly got paid down by the same amount by a random donor."

Ian stayed quiet, guilty as charged.

"And I got a part-time job to pay you back, but then what happened?" she continued.

She stared at him, looking like she was waiting for him to speak.

"Got nothing to say?" she finally asked, her toe tapping on the wood flooring.

"I have plenty, but what's the use? You're too stubborn to hear it."

7

Ian might be stubborn. He might be bull-headed. But he'd met his match in Daphne Thompson. When it came to digging heels in, she took the cake.

"You kept at it. Didn't you?" Daphne pressed.

"You're acting like I tried to steal from you, instead of offering a little assistance," he defended.

"Did I ever ask for it?" she continued, the toe making double time.

"No. Never," he stated. He would know because quite a few others in their class tried to buddy up to him to be best friends with or date a Firebrand. He'd been on a couple of dates where the person he was out with called him by one of his brothers' names. To some, it didn't matter which Firebrand they dated, as long as they dated one.

"Some folks would construe that as an insult, Ian," she said.

"Since you're remembering this all these years later, help me understand why that was a bad thing." He truly wanted to know what he'd done wrong.

"I didn't earn or deserve the money," she said flatly. He

could always count on her to come out straight with whatever was on her mind. It was one of her many good qualities —qualities that he missed.

"Neither did I," he said as honestly as he could. It was true. "I was born and then I had a bank account, Daphne. I didn't work for it and—"

"You might not have before you could walk, but you've worked the ranch and gone to school. Balancing being on the high school basketball team with calving season. You definitely deserve every penny," she said, cutting him off.

Before he could respond, his cell buzzed. He checked the screen.

"Dr. Ynez is pulling up. You might want to quiet the Dobermans and keep them in the next room while he checks out Henry," Ian said.

"They're fine as long as I'm in the room," she said. "Unless the doctor wouldn't be comfortable with them around."

"Unless you've forgotten, most folks around here are used to animals," he said, then thought he probably shouldn't have been so blunt.

"Right. It's not like I moved out of the state, Ian," she quipped, shooting him a stare right back.

"You might as well have," he said low and under his breath as he moved toward the door. He unlocked it, thinking six months ago no one in this town would have done this. Folks would have left their keys in their vehicle and the engine running if they needed to run a quick errand. Times changed. People changed. The only constant was change. And there'd been more crime in Lone Star Pass since the Marshall had died than in the town's entire history.

Ian opened the door as Dr. Ynez parked his Range Rover.

The good doctor exited the vehicle, grabbed something out of the backseat Ian assumed was a medical bag, and made a beeline for the front door.

Dr. Ynez was six-feet-tall, average height for Texans, with a runner's build. In fact, he took time off regularly to run marathons.

"Thank you for coming on such short notice," Ian said to the doctor, taking his outstretched hand. Ynez was in his late fifties but looked much younger. His hair grayed at the temples and that was the only real sign the man was aging.

"You're welcome, Ian. You mentioned a nine-year-old boy with a fever," Ynez got right to the point.

"That's right. Follow me," he said, turning around and leading the doctor into the downstairs guestroom where Daphne sat on the edge of the bed. "You've met Daphne Thompson."

"I have had the pleasure. It's good to see you again," Ynez said as he pulled gloves from this pocket and slipped them on foregoing a handshake in favor of getting down to business.

"This is my son Henry," she said to the doctor. "He's nine years old and had a fever when Ian called. It's down now after Advil, but he was complaining of a sore throat."

"Does he have a history of throat infections?" Ynez continued. "Swollen tonsils?"

"No. He's really healthy. There have been two episodes of strep in the past three years," she informed him.

"That's a low number for a child his age," Ynez's tone said he approved.

"He hasn't been around other kids as much as I'd like, so that probably helped," she stated.

Ynez nodded.

"I'll just wake him up for you, so you can give him an

exam," she stated, gently touching Henry's arm and saying his name. "Sweetie, wake up for Mommy."

Henry complied with her request but never fully opened his eyes. At least, not until the rapid strep test was administered. Then, he gagged a couple of times with eyes wide open. By the time the doctor was finished a few minutes later, Henry was already halfway back to dreamland.

"Is there a place I can set up in the kitchen while we wait out the few minutes before the test results come back?" Dr. Ynez asked. He removed his gloves and tucked them inside a plastic bag before sliding it in the side pocket of his medical bag.

DAPHNE LOOKED TO IAN. "Would you mind? I'd like to stay here with Henry a few more minutes while we wait. Let me know if my dad wakes up, will you?"

"Not a problem at all," Ian responded. "Doc, if you'd like to follow me this way, I'll lead you to it."

As the pair left the room, Daphne was starting to realize just how much coming home would change her and Henry's lives. For Henry's sake, she was thrilled he would finally get to know his father. It was about time. She couldn't count the number of times she'd wished for this exact thing, Henry and his father to be close. It was beginning to dawn on her that she was going to have to learn to be more flexible and let Ian become more involved. He deserved that and so much more. She hated that the Marshall had taken Henry away from Ian. At eighteen, she couldn't stand up to the man. Now, she realized that maybe she'd had more leverage with him than she'd ever realized. She watched her sleeping baby for a few minutes before taking in a deep breath.

Being around Ian again stirred up so many good memories. The last kisses they'd shared were the best she'd ever experienced, bar none. Not one kiss in the past decade could measure up. There was so much more than physical attraction between them, although that was strong too. They had chemistry like she'd never known before or since.

Daphne pushed off the bed before moving into the kitchen.

The doctor had set up a small station on the counter near the sink with the rapid strep test kit. She'd seen the swab before, but the small petri dish reminded her of something she would have used in high school biology lab.

"How's it going in here?" she asked as the doctor stared at the dish.

"Good," he said without turning. "In fact, it's looking like good news indeed."

"No strep?" she asked.

"Looks like we're dealing with a virus. I saw drainage in Henry's throat, which is most likely the culprit for the sore throat and caused by the virus," he continued. A few seconds later, the kit was cleaned up and he'd turned to face her. "Let me know if the fever gets worse or if any other new symptoms show up. My guess is that he needs to ride this out over the next five to seven days. Ibuprofen should handle the fever just fine. I expect it will break on its own in a couple of days anyway if not by morning."

Those words were a relief.

"As you know, antibiotics won't do anything to help a virus," he continued.

She nodded in agreement. From the corner of her eye, she saw Ian studying the doctor like he was cramming for finals. Yeah, her heart was taking a hit and life was changing all the way around in so many ways than she'd considered when she first made the decision to come home. But then, there hadn't been a decision to make. Taking care of her father was a no-brainer.

But could she keep Ian at a safe distance? And did she want to? Because despite all the years in between, it seemed that he had the power to crush her all over again.

IAN THANKED THE DOCTOR, before walking him out the front door. The sun was rising on the eastern horizon and the air was cooling just enough to let him know the intense summer heat was waning.

The reassurance from Ynez there wasn't anything seriously wrong with Henry should ease Ian's fears. He was learning as a new father it didn't exactly work that way. His muscles were strung so tight a cellist could play them despite the knowledge Henry would be fine.

Ian waved to the good doctor as he drove off, then made a beeline for the front door, locked it, then headed straight to the kitchen where Daphne was putting on a fresh pot of coffee.

"How do you do it?" he asked.

She turned around and placed the palms of her hands on the bullnose countertop. "You should have seen me when he was little. I would just hold this tiny little baby in my arms while fear practically consumed me, wondering how I was going to do it."

"I know we can't go back and I don't live in the past, but I would have liked to see him as a baby," Ian said.

"Well, I do have the next best thing." She held up a finger before retrieving her cell phone.

The coffee machine beeped, so he told her he'd pour the

cups as she flipped through her phone. Daphne took a seat at the table as he brought over the caffeine boosts. He sat down and put one of the mugs near her, unable to deny how much the world had felt out of balance in the past ten years of showing up here to help Mr. Thompson without her presence. There was a whole lot of frustration on his part when it came to the old man keeping this big of a secret from him, but Daphne was his only child and she'd asked him to not to mention the baby to anyone back home.

"Your dad never put up a picture of Henry or you anywhere around the house," Ian finally said as she scrolled.

"First of all, in his defense, he didn't know Henry belonged to you," she said, repeating what he already knew.

"Believe it or not, that makes me feel better about my relationship with him," Ian said. "Still, no new pictures and no mention in ten years."

"When is the last time you put out a new picture in your house?" she asked.

"Fair point. I pretty much leave everything alone," he said.

"Did you ever talk about me?" she asked.

"No," he stated. The subject had been off limits in an unspoken sense.

"Okay, so I specifically asked my father not to mention me or Henry around you," she said. "I told him that I broke up with you and I didn't think you would appreciate the reminder of me."

"Wasn't he suspicious of the timing of Henry's birth?" he asked. "I don't know much about kids and pregnancy but I would think your father could put two-and-two together."

"I didn't tell him right away," she said. "When Henry came, I told him that I didn't know who the father was, so he would keep my secret. He wouldn't want people in town to look down on me and having a so-called bastard child would definitely ignite the gossip mill."

"By the time you told him, enough time had probably passed," he reasoned.

She nodded.

"It still hurts," he said out loud, not meaning to.

"Yeah? I just hope you know who to take it out on," she quipped. "The Marshall did this when he threatened I'd never see my child again if I didn't leave town. I even faltered because I couldn't imagine living one day without you in my life. You weren't just my boyfriend. You were my best friend, Ian."

"Understood," he said.

"When I said as much to him, he gave the threat about taking away my father's livelihood," she said.

Ian shook his head. It was clear the memory was painful for her based on the tension lines on her face. Anger filled him at the thought he couldn't confront his grandfather. Was there any life at the Firebrand ranch the Marshall didn't try to interfere with, damage, or outright ruin?

"I don't have to tell you how much this business means to my dad. You know as well as I do it was all he had aside from me when my mom left after having the affair," she said. "The scarlet letter she wore for months after made it impossible for her to stay here." Tears streamed down Daphne's face now. "She wrote me once and said I would be a whole lot better off without her in my life. That she would ruin my reputation and drag me down with her. She believed that too. There was no return address so I couldn't even have it out with her. I didn't get the chance to convince her that I didn't care about what others thought."

"Some folks in this town could be cruel back then with

their sharp tongues," he said. The gossip mill was still alive and strong. And, yes, there were those who were happiest when they were meddling in other people's business. But most folks who lived here were understanding and kind. This wasn't the moment to point any of that out to Daphne.

"You think?" More of those tears streamed down her cheeks. Tears he wanted to reach over and thumb away but touching her was even more dangerous to his heart and it had already taken a beating today.

"I'm sorry, Daphne," was all he could say.

"I know you are," she responded in a voice that stirred his heart. She was the strongest person he knew, and he admired the hell out of her for her strength. She would see her tears as weakness but that was nothing but being strong for too long leaking out of her eyes.

Setting good sense aside, Ian leaned over and thumbed away a tear anyway. He let his hand linger on the creamy skin of her face. "I'm glad your father called me to help yesterday."

She sniffled a couple of times before nodding.

"So am I," she finally said.

They both stood at the same time and he brought her into his arms. She looped her arms around his neck and he lowered his head, resting his forehead on hers.

"You're amazing, Daphne," he said in practically a whisper. "You've done an amazing job with our son."

"Thank you, Ian," she said and she was almost breathless. When she tilted her head up to look in his eyes, it was all he could do not to kiss her. Kissing Daphne would be bad no matter how right it felt in the moment. The moment would soon be gone and where would that leave them? Their relationship was already complicated enough. They didn't need to confuse it with something from the past.

Technically, they didn't even know each other as adults. They'd been nothing but kids when they'd last been together. Time changed people.

And yet standing there, looking into her eyes, it was like time warped and he got stuck in the wave. They were eighteen again and in love. So much so, they'd decided to take their relationship to the next level. They'd made love. Despite their inexperience, sex with anyone but Daphne had never measured up since.

Was it the reason he saw himself as a lifelong bachelor? It wasn't in Ian's blood to settle for something less than the best.

The question dissipated in the fog surrounding his brain from being this close to the love of his life. *At one time* she'd been the love of his life, he corrected. Now, he was meeting her for the first time as nearly thirty-year-olds. Each with their own battle scars.

Before he fell down the rabbit hole of needing to be with Daphne, he took in a breath and let her go. He cleared his throat in an attempt to find his voice again.

"We should look at those pictures," he said, turning toward the table and searching for the phone. He needed to concentrate on something besides the sexy cupid's bow above her full, thick lips or how right her body had felt pressed against his. Or despite their considerable height difference how they fit each other perfectly. And he definitely shouldn't think about how her sexy curves would feel as he trailed his finger down her hip.

8

Daphne's mouth was so dry, she felt like she was dying of thirst in the Sahara. And Ian was her oasis. She took a sip of coffee to ease some of the dryness. The sound of a vehicle pulling up outside gave her a jolt of adrenaline. She glanced at the clock on the kitchen wall.

"It's probably the alarm company," she said, moving to the living room to check. From the window, she recognized the Firebrand Ranch truck. "What's Bronc doing here?"

"That would be my fault," Ian said as he joined her. Then he put his hands in the surrender position, palms up. "I hope I didn't overstep my bounds again, but I asked him to bring over a few items I thought might keep this place more secure."

"When it comes to keeping Henry safe, there are no more boundaries," she stated.

"You asked me to take him to the ranch before. I know I didn't give you an answer," he said. "This is my response, because I don't think Henry would do well without the one person who has made him feel safe his entire life. I think he needs to be home with his mother, and I'd like to stick around until you deem it's safe for me to leave."

"That is thoughtful of you, Ian." The sweet sentiment caused a knot to form in her chest.

"No problem, Daphne. I mean it. You've done all the heavy lifting with our son so far and I'd like ease your load," he said as he unlocked the door. "Plus, I don't think it's best for mine and Henry's relationship for him to be forced to be around me on our own. I'd like to take our time getting to know each other."

"I agree that would be best," she said.

Ian gave a quick nod of approval, flashed a smile that threatened to melt all her defenses, and then headed outside. Bronc was exiting the truck and despite ten years passing he looked the same as always. He had to be in his mid- to late-sixties by now with that same weather-worn skin and permanent tan. His forehead used to have a perpetual worry line etched in it when she was a kid and it didn't seem like much had changed from this distance at least.

Daphne returned to the kitchen and finished off her coffee before rummaging through the fridge. There wasn't much to work with here. She grabbed a piece of paper and pen from the living room before jotting down grocery store on her list of things to do. Having Ian here would make life a whole lot simpler. She would be able to run errands without worrying something would happen to Henry while she was gone. Being able to leave once in a while would give her some sense of normalcy.

Her dad looked surprisingly good last night despite the diagnosis. She did realize the word 'rapid' meant his condition would change quickly. It was hard to fathom her father declining. He'd always been so strong. Her rock.

The cupboard was bare, which meant there was nothing to fix for breakfast. As she checked on Henry, she heard her father coming downstairs. Considering the night Henry had had, he probably wouldn't wake for another couple of hours at a minimum. Luis and Luna were stretched out on the carpet next to Henry's side of the bed. This seemed like a good time to slip away and grab some groceries. She kissed Henry's forehead before leaving the room, closed the doors behind her to contain Luis and Luna in the bedroom, and made a beeline for the kitchen. Since they'd met her father on several occasions since she bought them, he'd be safe around them. The brilliance of that move was beginning to show now that she would be living with her father. The Dobermans loved him.

"Hey, Dad. Good morning," she said to her father.

He gasped before spinning around to see who was there. It was like he didn't recognize his daughter's voice.

"It's me. Daphne," she said, stopping at the entrance.

"Right. Good morning," Dad said and recognition seemed to dawn. She noticed how quickly he'd tried to cover his reaction, and thought how awful it must be to realize he was losing his memories of people, places, and of his life. The thought of losing all the memories that made a person who they were and comforted them as they looked back on the life they had built must be overwhelming at times.

Daphne was still trying to process what the next couple of years might look like. No matter what, she would be there for the man who'd raised her, loved her, and had done nothing but care for her. She wouldn't forgive the Marshall for taking away the last years she had with her dad despite never wanting to speak ill of the dead.

Looking back, she'd known there was no choice but to

leave Lone Star Pass and the only family she'd known. She'd kept in touch with her dad, calling every few days to check in and meeting him halfway for dinners until she couldn't hide the pregnancy any longer. More of that anger surfaced at the missed time together.

At least she was here now when it counted, she decided. And no one, not even Miles, got to take this away from her again.

"I need to run out to pick up some groceries," she said to her dad.

"Why is that?" he asked, motioning toward the window.

She walked over and caught sight of Bronc and Ian carrying boxloads of what looked like food. They were coming in the back door, so she unlocked the back and wedged a chair under the handle to keep it open for them.

If she walked in the living room and checked his memo pad, she would no doubt find groceries listed. Ian's generosity knew no bounds and she decided it was best not to fight it.

"Thought we could barbecue steaks on the grill tonight," Ian said as he brought in a boxload of food. "That okay with everyone else?"

"You won't hear any complaints from me," Dad said with an ear-to-ear grin.

"Your father was worried about not having enough food for you and Henry when you came. I told him I would handle it," Ian whispered to Daphne after she joined him at the table where he set down his box. "Mentioning it to you yesterday slipped my mind. I apologize if—"

"Don't," she said, touching his arm. "It's very sweet of you to help out my dad like this."

Ian flashed the same smile that released a dozen butter-flies in her stomach every time since elementary school.

Even then she'd known he was someone special. She just didn't know how much or how big of an impact he would have on her life.

The sound of gravel crunching underneath tires drew her attention back to the window.

"That must be the alarm company," she said. She checked and saw the company logo on the vehicle. "I'll just get him started unless you guys need me."

"No. Go on. I'll get breakfast going, with the help of your dad," Ian stated.

Daphne was not used to having this level of help. She could definitely get used to it, she thought, as she walked outside. She passed Bronc, stopping long enough to give him a hug and thank him for showing up with all the food and supplies. He waved it off like it was nothing, but the gesture meant so much to her that more of those hot tears threatened to leak from her eyes.

After introducing herself to the alarm company rep, Todd, she showed him around the place as he assessed their highest risk points.

Back at his vehicle, she had the prickly feeling someone was watching her. Her gaze flew to the kitchen window but no one was standing there and the strange sensation had been coming from behind her anyway, back by the trees.

"I'll take whatever full protection you have to offer, keeping in mind that the dogs stay inside the house," she said.

"No motion sensors then," Todd stated.

"Nope," she said.

He went into a lengthy monologue about window breaking sensors and the benefits of using cellular versus the old-fashioned landline for the system. She nodded before turning him loose so he could install the system.

When she stepped back inside the kitchen, the smell of bacon caused her stomach to growl. It was already quarter to eight.

"Where is the morning going?" she asked as she refilled her coffee cup. Her dad was still in the kitchen but Ian and Bronc got up and left out the front door once Todd started doing his bit.

"Sit down and I'll fix you a plate of eggs and bacon," Dad said.

"It smells amazing," she said. "Mind if I check on Henry first?"

"Go right ahead," Dad said. "I'll keep your plate warm."

Daphne was relieved her dad was none the wiser about all the activity downstairs in the middle of the night. He had enough to worry about with his own medical condition. She didn't want to add to his burden.

Luis and Luna needed to go outside for a potty break and eat breakfast soon. They were sitting up, ears on high alert, no doubt not loving all the activity. Henry, however, was still asleep. His forehead felt fine, which was a huge relief.

"Ready to eat?" she asked the Dobermans. Neither got up. They must not want to leave Henry's side yet. Since he would be up soon, she figured they would be all right staying put a little while longer. At least until Todd needed to put sensors on the guest room window. Speaking of which, it was the only downstairs bedroom. She would have her work cut out for her convincing her dad to switch but not having to go upstairs would be easier on him. There was enough change in her dad's life right now. She would leave that topic alone for the time being.

She closed the door behind her, leaving it just cracked

enough to hear if Henry called for her. Halfway to the kitchen, her father shouted.

IAN HEARD the distress in Mr. Thompson's voice from the yard. He bolted toward the backdoor and into the kitchen in time to see a confused-looking man standing in the kitchen. The alarm guy?

"Dad, I told you about Todd coming here this morning to install an alarm system," Daphne was explaining. The Dobermans started barking and a startled Henry came running into the room no doubt in search of his mother. Waking up in a strange place probably had him confused as well.

"What? Why?" Mr. Thompson dropped the plate in his hand, and it went tumbling to the floor.

"I got this," Ian said, moving quick to grab cleaning supplies. Thankfully, the plates weren't the breakable kind, or there would be twice the mess. He took a knee as Daphne tried to calm her dad.

"It's all good, Dad," she soothed as Henry wrapped his arms around her waist. He buried his face in her side.

Todd backed up against the wall as the Dobermans locked onto him. Daphne issued a command in what sounded like German, and they sat down on the spot. Good dogs. Ian hoped he could be worked into their training for when Henry came to the ranch. The dogs wouldn't do well without Henry, and Ian figured the feeling would be mutual. They, along with Daphne, were the only constants in Henry's life.

"Sorry," Daphne said to Todd. "Would you be able to work in another room until we're able to clear the kitchen?"

"Yes, ma'am," Todd stated. His gaze flew to the dogs. "Will they let me do my job?"

"I'm about to take them outside," Daphne stated, walking Henry toward the table.

"Hey, Mr. Thompson. Mind if I have a cup of coffee?" Ian asked. He could get it himself, but Mr. Thompson would volunteer to pour it and that would give him something to do.

"I'll get it for you," Daphne's dad said. He turned around and grabbed a mug from the cabinet like chaos hadn't just happened.

Daphne flashed eyes at Ian and mouthed the words *thank you.* She walked the Dobermans to the back door and then took them outside with Henry clinging for dear life to her waist. She managed to put out bowls of food and water while Henry kept his spindly arms wrapped around her.

The mess didn't take long to clean. By the time Mr. Thompson turned around, Ian was dumping the bacon and eggs in the trash. He grabbed and wetted a couple of paper towels so he could wipe the floor.

"Here you go," Mr. Thompson said, handing over a mug the second Ian was finished.

"Thank you," Ian said, realizing the uphill climb Daphne was going to have in taking care of her father, her son, and trying to keep safe from the bastard who had her on the run these past two years.

"Do you have time to stay for a bit?" Mr. Thompson asked, not seeming to realize Ian had been there since the night before.

"If it's all right with you, I'd like to stay on here for a few days." Ian figured this was as good a window as any. Mr. Thompson might not remember this conversation, but Ian would give the elder gentleman the benefit of the doubt. If that didn't work out, he would repeat the request.

"Fine by me," Mr. Thompson said with a smile. "I'll just let Daphne know."

"Thank you, sir," Ian said. "I better go help Bronc outside."

"Well, all right. Thanks for stopping by," Mr. Thompson said.

On the way out, Ian received a call from the family accountant.

"Hey, Manny. How's the family?" Ian asked.

"We're all good here," Manny said. "How about you and yours?"

"I'm learning something new every day about mine," Ian said. "But we're doing all right."

"I got your text," Manny started. There was hesitation in his tone.

"What is it?" Ian asked.

"I'm good with setting up a trust in Daphne Thompson's name but wouldn't it be easier to add money to the million dollars your grandfather had me set up almost ten years ago?" Manny asked.

"What?" Ian asked, hoping he hadn't heard right.

"The account set up by your grandfather," Manny repeated. "Do you want a new account or should I add money to that one?"

"Do you still have access?" Ian asked, wondering how much was left. Daphne's Jeep wasn't new. Had she blown through the money already? Was that the real reason she left Lone Star Pass and kept Ian's child from him? The Marshall paid her off? Ian didn't want to believe his ears. She'd made no mention of the funds when she'd listed off the reasons for leaving town and not telling him about the pregnancy. In his experience, liars withheld information. Honest people had nothing to hide.

"Deposit only," Manny stated.

"Good to know," Ian said. "Let me think about it and get back to you."

"Sounds good," Manny said. "I can do it either way. No problem."

"Thank you," Ian said before saying goodbyes and ending the call. A million dollars was nothing to sneeze at. Why had Daphne left that part out of the equation? Did she think he wouldn't find out? She gotten downright offended at him for offering financial help. From the looks of it, her and Henry had struggled to make ends meet. Why wouldn't she fess up to the money?

Ian sat on the information as he helped Bronc install the cameras and the motion detector lights. They moved methodically to each corner of the house and then first floor windows. The flash of light would cause the camera to click a picture. He would know if anyone tried to move around the perimeter of the home. The alarm would add a second layer of defense. If—and that was a big if—someone breached the home, Ian would be waiting on the inside along with Daphne and the Dobermans. The biggest threat to anyone determined enough to get inside the house came from a mother bear protecting her cub.

From the corner of his eye, he saw Henry and the Dobermans heading toward him. The little boy carried two bottles of water in his hands.

"Excuse me, sir." Henry stopped at the base of the ladder as Ian worked to install a motion-detecting light above the kitchen window.

"You can call me Ian." Dad didn't sound right since the

two had just met, but Ian did want his son to call him something less formal.

"Mr. Ian, would you like a bottle of water?" Henry asked in the most earnest tone.

Well, at least the kid wasn't calling Ian *sir*. He'd take the progress. He climbed down from the ladder and sat on one of the steps, bringing him closer to Henry's height. "You could just call me Ian if you'd like."

"Okay." Henry handed over a cold bottle. Ian pressed it to his forehead. The move reminded him how hot Henry's had looked in the middle of the night. "How are you feeling today?"

Henry shrugged. "Better, but Mom won't let me run around outside." The disappointment in his tone would make a person think he'd just had all his candy stolen without the possibility of ever getting more.

Ian took a sip of water.

"We have a horse on the ranch name Luna," he said. "It's a good name."

"You have a horse?" Henry's eyes grew wide when he asked and Ian tried not be upset with Daphne at how little Henry knew about his own father.

"We have a whole barn full of 'em," Ian stated. The kid's eyes opened even wider if that was possible. "You and your mom are welcome to visit the ranch any time you like. We have a huge barn and more animals running around than I can count. Plus, the yard goes on as far as the eye can see."

"Really?" The wonder in Henry's voice made Ian see the world through innocent eyes. It was sweet and reminded him to appreciate the little things in life.

His mind snapped back to the money and the fact Daphne hadn't mentioned it to him, and he couldn't help the feeling of betrayal.

9

By dinner, Daphne had managed to keep Henry inside other than the few times he'd asked to bring something to Ian, and his fever down. She was grateful on both counts. Her father went about his routine. It was the same as it had been more than a decade ago. Morning coffee and breakfast followed by puttering around the house. He'd exchanged a print newspaper in favor of reading on a tablet. Once he got a 'sense of the day' as he said, he headed outside to the barn then tended to the bees.

The alarm system had been installed. She'd unpacked several boxes and put a few personal touches around the house. There was much to do but this was progress. The U-Haul had to go back tomorrow but she would consider this day a success.

Ian had stayed outside most of the day. He was already lighting up the grill by the time she sat down with her second pot of coffee for the day, Henry resting his head on the pillow positioned on her lap.

It was a luxury to be able to sit down with him; she would normally be in the kitchen, making dinner. With Ian manning the grill and her father pitching in, there wasn't much for her to do to get ready for dinner after feeding the Dobermans. She reminded herself not to get too used to this. Once the threat had passed, and she could only pray it would soon for Henry's sake, Ian would go back to the ranch and she would step up her father's care.

Maybe she could even enroll Henry at the same elementary school she'd gone to what felt like a hundred years ago. She had never ever allowed herself to consider the thought he might spend the last nine years of his childhood growing up in the same house she did. Her heart squeezed at the thought as she absently stroked Henry's hair with one hand while balancing a cup of coffee on the sofa with the other. This was her version of heaven on earth. All the men she loved under one roof. Yes, she loved Ian. Her feelings for him had never been in question. She'd loved him enough to leave town so he could have a future, even though it had felt like her heart had been ripped out of her chest.

Right now, all she wanted to think about was being here in this house with her son, her father, and her best friend. She still wasn't certain when Bronc had taken off.

"Dinner's ready." Her dad popped his head in the living room. "Ian is cooking up the fatted cow, so I hope you guys are hungry."

Henry perked up at the mention of Ian.

"We'll be right there after we wash our hands," Daphne said to her father.

"Your friend said I could come to his ranch anytime I wanted," Henry said on the way to the hall bathroom. He'd cheered up considerably at the mention of her friend.

"That was nice of him," Daphne said.

"They have horses and cows and dogs everywhere." The admiration on Henry's face reminded her just how much he loved animals. He'd always preferred camping trips to hotels, and she'd used his fondness a time or two when they needed a quick escape. Pitching a tent at a campground worked anytime besides summer in Texas. She couldn't take the melt the rubber soles of her shoes on pavement heat, despite living here for her entire life.

"I've been to the Firebrand Ranch. It's a spectacular place," Daphne said to a much-impressed Henry. She smiled. "Ian has eight brothers and nine cousins, all boys."

"Whoa!" Henry exclaimed.

"I know, right?" She would find a way to explain to him that he was part of that family too now, and that Ian would be part of Henry's life. "I'm really glad you like my friend, Henry."

"He's nice," Henry said with a bright smile. It was difficult to convince a kid like him to stay inside when he felt this great. The heat would wear him down fast though and she'd convinced him cartoons on the couch were better than running through the grass, pulling off a minor miracle.

"Yes, he is." She remembered how much Ian loved being outdoors; like father, like son. If Henry turned out to be half the man Ian proved to be, she would consider herself lucky.

Henry finished washing up and dried his hands.

"Ready?" she asked. Kids fevers could spike so quickly and then drop just as fast. It was the most remarkable thing how they were able to bounce back from sickness. She prayed she wouldn't catch whatever he'd had. On her, it would look a whole lot different.

"Yes," Henry beamed.

She walked him into the kitchen where her father sat at the table with a plate of steak, grilled asparagus, and a baked potato with the works. Forget eating a bowl of greens, she was all in for this meal.

Glancing around, she noticed Ian stayed outside with his plate. He sat on a lounge chair, balancing his plate on his knee.

"Henry, why don't you stay here with Pops and I'll give our friend Ian some company," she said.

"Okay." Henry shrugged before taking his seat. He had always been an easy child.

Much to Daphne's shock, Luis and Luna were out back with Ian. How on earth did he win them over?

She fixed Henry's plate and then hers before heading out the back door. A quick survey made her feel better about sitting down. "Mind if I eat with you?"

Ian didn't look up. "Suit yourself."

His expression said something had happened. But what? He'd been here all day working. They'd barely spoken to each other.

"I can go inside if you'd rather," she said.

"It wouldn't hurt my feelings," he shot back.

Wounded by the comment, Daphne turned around and headed back inside the kitchen. "Change of plans. I'd rather be in here with the two of you."

"Pops and me were just planning our escape," Henry said.

"Pops and I," Daphne corrected as she took a seat, bemused and trying to shake off the snub from Ian.

"No," Henry stated with authority. "Pops and *me*."

Daphne smiled. She couldn't help it. Some battles were best fought at another time and place. "And when do you plan to do this?"

"It wouldn't be a secret if I told you," Henry said with his best *duh* voice.

"We were just talking nonsense," Dad said, waving at thin air.

"Where were you planning to go?" she asked, trying to keep a playful tone but her concern level raised at the way her dad was trying to sweep this under the rug.

"Camping in the woods," Henry stated.

"All by yourself?" Daphne played along.

"No, silly. We're taking Luis and Luna. They'll keep us safe. Right, Pops?" Henry was so proud of their plans. Daphne, on the other hand, was concerned.

The rest of the meal was spent in small talk. Daphne did all the dishes but the one in Ian's hand. He didn't seem ready to come inside and she'd learned to give him space a long time ago. He came around eventually when he was ready to talk. She hoped he hadn't changed because learning her father had been talking about escaping had sent her into a stress tailspin.

"Let's get you in a warm bath," Daphne said to Henry.

"Can I shower instead?" he asked.

"Sure." She tousled his hair. "But you usually love your baths. What's different tonight?"

"Shower is faster," he said.

"Why are you in such a hurry?" she asked as she walked him to the bathroom.

"I have to pack," he said. Her heart sank. Did her father plan to 'escape' soon? Like tonight? Or was it just talk?

"You can't go anywhere until you're all well," she said. "Doctor's orders."

Henry groaned.

"Get in there and make sure you wash everywhere," she said, thinking she needed to have a conversation with her father.

Once Henry was all set, she moved back to the kitchen.

"Hey, Dad. Was there anything I should be concerned about in the conversation from Henry?" she asked.

"I don't know what you're talking about," Dad said as he messed around in the kitchen. "Coffee?"

"Another cup can't hurt." As it was, the lack of sleep from the last couple of nights was starting to wear thin.

"No, it can't." Dad whistled while he went through the ritual. At least he didn't skip any steps. He remembered how to make coffee. It might seem like a small thing but there would come a time, according to the doctor, when even this would be a puzzle to her dad. There was no way to prepare herself for that time. Thinking about it wouldn't make it any less painful. For now, she tabled the heavy thought.

Ian walked into the room and the air chilled so much she would need the cup of coffee for warmth. What had she done wrong?

"Coffee?" Mr. Thompson asked as Ian stepped inside the kitchen.

"Yes. Thank you." He was grateful to have company besides Daphne in the room. The two of them needed to talk at some point, but this didn't seem like the right time.

Mr. Thompson poured three mugs and handed them over, serving himself last. "I like to take mine on the front porch."

"Okay, Dad." There was more than a hint of worry in Daphne's voice as her father nodded and then left the room. A moment later, the front door opened and closed.

Ian started toward the back door.

"What did I do to upset you?" Daphne asked. "I mean...today."

Before he could answer, Henry came bopping into the room.

"Can I watch TV?" he asked.

"Yes. Let me turn on your show." She disappeared into the next room and returned a few moments later. The low hum of the TV echoed into the cozy kitchen.

Coffee in one hand, her balled fist on her hip, she asked the same question as a few minutes ago before Henry interrupted them.

"Nothing," he said. "You didn't do anything *today* to upset me."

"What's that supposed to mean?" she quipped.

"I said it wasn't today," he stated.

"You can be mad at me all you want for what happened a decade ago. I don't expect you to get over everything because we're back in town and showed up in your life, but I—"

"What did you do with the money, Daphne?"

"The what?" She shot him a warning look.

"The million dollars from the Marshall," he said. "Did your ex spend it all? Did he buy drugs? Blow through it? Is that why it's all gone and you're driving my son around in a Jeep that has seen better days. Couldn't you at least have thought of Henry's well-being enough to buy something safer? Or did you give the money to some random guy you met to get his band started or keep it on the road?"

"Are you serious right now?" she asked, anger causing her cheeks to flame. He could always tell the degree based on just how red they got. At this point, he'd say she would blow in less than five minutes.

"Do I look like I'm joking?" he quipped. "You wanted to know. I told you. What's the matter? You can't handle it when I call you out?"

Daphne took in a breath like she did when she was trying to keep her blood pressure from boiling over. She walked over to the counter and he noticed it was the farthest distance from Henry.

"What's the matter? Don't you want your son to know that you blew through money that should have been set aside for his future?" he pressed, his own mercury rising to a dangerous level. "It's one thing to take my son away from me. It's another to *keep* him away from me. But to take money from my grandfather and pretend you left to save me, or your father just—"

"What?" She stood there, tapping her toe on the tile floor.

Rather than continue down a road that would only lead to more heartache, he said, "I thought I knew you better, Daphne. Turns out, I don't know you at all."

"Are you done?" she asked with an infuriatingly steady voice.

Ian took a sip of coffee. He probably didn't need the boost considering anger had him riled up already, but he figured it couldn't hurt at this point.

"Now, I'm done," he said.

Daphne set her mug down and made a beeline for him. She poked her index finger in the middle of his chest. "How dare you, Ian Firebrand."

He started to open his mouth to argue but she shushed him with one look. He knew that look. It was the one that said he'd just been a class-A jerk and was about to get his behind handed to him. Few people ever went up against Ian Firebrand. In fact, he could count the number on one hand. Daphne Thompson was one of those people. And he realized he was about to be dressed down.

"I was afraid of your grandfather. I was scared in general. And I was alone," she said, with anger sparking in those honest blue eyes of hers. "Maybe I shouldn't have believed he would take me to court and ensure that I would never see my son again as long as I live. Maybe I shouldn't have believed one of the most powerful men in Texas would ruin my father's mom and pop honey shop. But I believed every word he said because he was a whole lot older than me and he was a whole lot richer than my family and we both know he squashed people like bugs if they got in his way."

"And the money?"

"I never asked for it and I never spent it, except to buy the Dobermans and pay for their training, which only cost a small portion of the interest. Henry can use it to pay for college and a buy a house when he gets older but I have never used a dime of it on me. And if you want the truth, I didn't even want to give the money to Henry because it feels dirty to me. Pay off money to ensure my son would never know his father," she said with her finger stabbing him in the chest every couple of beats.

Well, now he really felt like a jerk. In fact, he probably should have guessed she would do something like that. She'd been back nearly twenty-four hours and he'd seen the amazing job she'd been doing with Henry.

Daphne was a good person. He'd let his anger take the wheel. And now, she looked ready to rip his head off. Rightfully so, he thought.

10

"I owe you an apology. All I can say is what we already know," Ian said to Daphne. "I wish you would have come to me."

"And then what? Your grandfather said he would have disinherited you," Daphne pointed out. Surely, he wasn't as naïve as he sounded right now. "I never would have risked your future or my father's."

Ian clenched his back teeth and she could see that his frustration was rising as the muscle in his jaw ticked. But was he still mad at her?

"I can prove that I never spent the money, except for the dogs and training," she continued. "I have the balance on an app on my phone."

"You don't need to do that, Daphne," he said after a sharp sigh. "I just wish the Marshall was still alive so I could..." He fisted his hands rather than finish the sentence and she knew that meant he would stop talking right there if she let him. He'd hold his emotions inside until they burst out.

"He isn't, Ian. So you need to find a way to forgive him

and move on, or this will eat you alive. Believe me, if hating him would help the situation I'd be right there with you. I'm angry too. He took away my father from me for the past ten years, and now I don't have a whole lot of time left when we should have years," she pointed out, fighting back the tears that came every time she thought about the situation.

Ian crossed his arms over a broad chest.

"You might have lost the past nine and a half years with Henry, but at least you have a future with him," she said. "If I was you, I wouldn't waste a minute of it looking back."

Ian's lips compressed and his gaze unfocused like he was looking inside himself for answers. It was a good sign she was getting through to him.

"If we keep going like this, we'll destroy any hope of a working relationship," she continued. "I, for one, am trying to put the past behind me, even though it's not always easy and I realize how much my own mistakes have cost the people I love."

Ian gave a slight nod.

"Now you know about the money," she said. "Honestly, I didn't realize it was important because I actively try to forget it's even there."

Ian stood there, quiet, for a long moment.

"I couldn't agree more about doing our best not to look backward. It's the fastest way for the future to kick this in the back of the head. I'm not saying it will be easy, but I'd like to try," he finally said. "As far as working together, I'd like to figure out how to get along and have the least negative impact on Henry."

Daphne nodded. "I can live with that, Ian. I hope you know that I always wanted you to be involved with your son. There has never been a time past or present that it was my desire to withhold him from you."

"Good. We'll start from there," he said. "Because Henry is a terrific kid. He needs his parents to get along and he deserves that from us."

"We're on the same team here, Ian," she stated. "No more secrets. I promise."

"I've seen the way the Marshall has destroyed our family. Before now, I didn't have anything against the man personally. If I'd known that he ran you out of town..." Ian seemed to need to rein in his emotions. "He was a master manipulator and I'm seeing the collateral damage. It's not the way I intend to live but it's real hard not to let my anger take hold."

"You saw what he did to your father and uncle," she stated. "He pitted me against the whole town and made me feel ashamed, scared."

"His influence ends now," Ian said. "And if you'll excuse me, I have a call to make."

"Are we good?" she asked, not bothering to mask her hope.

"I am. You?" he asked.

She nodded, resisting the urge to push up to her tiptoes and seal the deal with a kiss.

Ian headed in the opposite direction as night fell.

CELL PHONE IN HAND, Ian had a call to make. More than one, to be honest, but he'd start there. He'd been born right in the middle of his cousins Travis and Vaughn. He'd been close with all of the Firebrands growing up, but none more so than Travis. Shame and regret filled Ian at the thought he hadn't reached out to his cousin after Travis's mother had been arrested for the attempted murder of Ian's newly minted sister-in-law and her grandmother. Ever since the Marshall's death, it seemed like there'd been a line drawn in the sand in between each side of the family and no one crossed it. Not even to offer words of encouragement, sympathy, or support.

The murder scandal had further divided the cousins, but the truth was that Travis hadn't had anything to do with it. Ian pulled up his cousin's name and contact information before touching the screen to make the call.

The call rolled into voicemail, so he left a message. Patching any of the relationships on either side of the family was going to take some doing, but he refused to let the Marshall win. Ian was more determined than ever to mend fences. Family should stick together.

His next call was to his brother Grayson.

"Hey, man," Grayson said. "Where are you?"

"Remember when you told me Daphne was back in town?" Ian asked, figuring he needed to introduce Henry into the family as soon as possible. Folks needed a minute to chew on information like this so by the time Henry came to the ranch, everyone would have adjusted to the idea of another grandkid around.

"Yes," he said. "It was more of a warning than anything else."

"Well, you don't have to worry about me running into her somewhere on accident," Ian stated.

"Why is that?" Grayson still hadn't caught on to what Ian was hinting about. To be fair, he was currently planning a royal wedding with the love of his life Kyra and, therefore, distracted.

"I'm here with her now," he stated.

"Oh. Okay. Good, right? That's good?" Grayson said, clearly stumbling over his words.

"She's in trouble," he continued. "There's a bad ex in the picture."

"Which is your problem because...?" Grayson asked, not hiding the irritation in his voice.

"We have a son," Ian stated as plain as day.

"How?" Grayson stammered. Then came, "No. Never mind. I know *how*. But, really...*how*?"

"His name is Henry and he's nine and a half years old," Ian said. He and Grayson were close and Ian had no doubt his brother would support him unconditionally.

"Wow. Congratulations, Ian." Grayson sounded genuine and like this was a curveball he wasn't expecting. "A son. That's a beautiful thing."

"I've only been around him for twenty-four hours, but I can already tell he's a special kid," Ian said.

"He's your and Daphne's child. He'd have to be special," Grayson said. "Did she say why she didn't tell you before now?"

Grayson of all people would understand complicated relationships. The family had worked their way quite a few since summer started, but they had lived their entire lives with Marshall Firebrand.

"Yes, and it's part of the reason I'm calling," Ian stated. "The Marshall scared her off, threatened her, and vowed to ruin her father's business if she stuck around."

Grayson muttered a curse.

"I never thought he meddled in my life before now," Ian stated. "Hearing her side of the story frustrates me to no end."

"I can only imagine," Grayson agreed. "Again, I'm sorry."

"Is this going to be our legacy, Grayson?" Ian asked. "We don't get along with the other side of the family. I know what Aunt Jackie did was all kinds of wrong, and I'm not suggesting we forgive her or forget that she tried to kill someone, but what about our cousins? We used to be close with the twins at one time. I was close with Travis and Vaughn. What happened?"

"I've been thinking the same things lately, man," Grayson admitted. "Our father and uncle's relationship might be toxic, but that shouldn't impact us."

"I do realize the Kellan and Liv situation, what with her marrying into our side of the family, complicates the potential for family reunions," Ian stated. "I'm not naïve to think we'll all hold hands and sing Kumbaya because I had an epiphany that our family should be close again."

"You're on the right track, though," Grayson stated. "Getting married has me thinking about who to invite. It would be easy to leave that whole side of the family out of the celebration. But I'm with you. When will it all end? We live on the same property for heaven's sake. Why are we drawing lines in the sand and daring each other to cross?"

"The inheritance complicates the situation," Ian said.

"I often wonder what our cousins think about Adam and Prudence claiming the Marshall's house," Grayson said. "We never even asked them if they wanted it."

"Technically, it belongs to our side of the family," Ian said. "But you're one hundred percent right about us taking what was given, without any regard for how that might make our uncle and cousins feel."

"My thoughts exactly," Grayson stated.

"We should set up a family meeting," Ian said. "Set the record straight once and for all."

"And what do you propose?" Grayson asked.

"We should split everything down the middle. Give them half the land, half the cattle, and half the property," Ian said. "Adam and Prudence can split the house too. Hell, there's an east and west wing. Or they can build a place of their own and we can use the old house for offices and when guests stay over. Think about it, our father isn't the same after the stroke. He needs to take a step back and let others run the business. Adam is a reasonable man. I think our brother will see the light once we explain our point of view even though he and Kellan have never gotten along. Times have changed and we need to change too."

"It could work," Grayson stated. "I'm not expecting a hundred percent agreement from our side of the family. Corbin has a lot of animosity toward Kellan for him courting Liv away."

"She ended up marrying Corbin after her divorce from Kellan, which was the right decision, by the way. I think we can all agree on that," Ian said.

"No one on our side of the family would argue. Not sure about our cousins," Grayson said.

"A fifty-fifty split is more than reasonable. They weren't going to get anything but mineral rights to land they don't own and, therefore, can never drill on. The current setup is lose-lose," Ian explained.

"I've thought of the same things and I believe most if not all of our brothers would say the same thing too," Grayson stated. "The grudge between our father and uncle goes way back. There might not be a bridge large enough to cover their divide. But we don't have to add to it."

"No. We might even have a chance to fix it, right?" Ian said. Maybe it was his new role as father that had him wanting peace in the family.

"How long will you be over at Daphne's place?" Grayson asked.

"Until there's no threat," Ian stated. "I don't have an exact timeframe."

"I'll see what I can do on my end over here," Grayson promised.

"Cool," Ian said, feeling good about putting wheels in motion. "But, hey, if you're needed for wedding planning just let me know and I'll see who else is available."

"Have you ever planned a royal wedding?" Grayson asked.

"You know I have not," Ian shot back, relieved at the lighter note in their conversation.

"Neither have I," Grayson teased. "I've given my future bride the reins. There are planners and protocols that are far above my head."

"Good idea to take a step back," Ian agreed.

"Hey, man. Congrats about your son," Grayson said on a more serious note. "It's a big deal and I know you're going to make a great father."

"I hope so," Ian admitted. "Henry's a great kid. He deserves nothing less in his dad."

"He couldn't have asked for a better man to be his dad." Grayson's vote of confidence made a dent in Ian's doubts.

"Thanks, man. I appreciate it," Ian said, and meant every word. His brother's opinion meant the world to Ian, reminding him how important family was to him and how putting in the work to bring theirs closer together could pay off big time.

"Any time," Grayson said. "Besides, it'll give me an excuse not to 'approve' flowers I've never even heard of." His brother laughed.

"It'll all be worth it when you and Kyra are official," Ian reminded.

"That is the gospel truth," Grayson agreed. "On a serious note, do you need an extra set of eyes at the Thompson house? Round the clock security?"

"Spread the word about Henry, if you don't mind. Let everyone know to watch out for strangers in town. Daphne has been in hiding for the past two years. I'm hoping the bastard has moved on at this point but we aren't taking anything for granted here. I have security out the wazoo."

"If anything changes, we're all here for you," Grayson said.

"You know I appreciate it," Ian said.

"I owe you for helping me with Kyra's situation, so I mean it. Call if you need anything," Grayson continued.

"Will do," Ian stated before saying goodbyes and ending the call. Knowing his brothers always had his back had gotten him through a whole lot in the past. Who did Daphne have in the past ten years? She couldn't ask her father. Hell, because of the Marshall, she hadn't even been able to come home.

It was a shame Henry wouldn't grow up with the same kind of support Ian had had. At the very least, the kid deserved two parents who got along and worked together for his best interest. Ian was going to have to figure out how to get past his hurt at all the lost years with his son. Being angry wouldn't do any good and it certainly wouldn't change anything.

Then there was Daphne to consider. She had enough on her plate without worrying about what Ian's next move might be.

None of this was how Ian had envisioned having a family. Granted, he hadn't thought much about it before this point. Now that he was, he thought it a terrible shame Henry would never have siblings.

And since this line of thinking was about as productive as trying to milk a daisy, he shoved the thoughts aside and moved on.

As he walked toward the house, motion off to his left caught his attention. He took a knee in case he needed to retrieve the gun in his ankle holster. The thought of anything happening to Daphne was a gut punch. He'd lost her once. There was no way it was happening again. Not if he had anything to say about it. He wouldn't survive it twice, especially now that she was back in his life.

11

"Show yourself," Ian demanded. The person wouldn't, but they would know he was aware of their presence. Then again, in these parts, it could be a wild boar or a black bear. The area was also known for dangerous coyotes. There were plenty of creatures as deadly as humans, none with the same premeditation skills.

The sound of leaves rustling in the opposite direction made him lean toward wild animal. Based on his experience as a tracker, a person would leave more quietly.

Just in case, he wouldn't take any chances. Ian drew his weapon and headed toward the noise. He kept as low a profile as he could, trying to make himself less of a target should someone be set up in the woods with a rifle. The noise could also be a decoy.

The sound of gravel crunching underneath someone's foot behind him had him spinning around, leading with his elbow. There was no one in sight. The U-Haul blocked his line of vision to the front door, which had him back peddling so he could get a clear visual on the front of the house.

Being out here on his own left him vulnerable to anyone with a scope who wanted to pick him off. Someone was definitely playing mind games with him and his first thought was the person or persons might be trying to draw him away from the house. So, rather than walk into a trap, he made a beeline for the front porch.

Ian made a mental note to move the U-Haul tomorrow. Out of nowhere, something that felt like a baseball bat slammed into him as he tried to come around the front of the U-Haul. Whatever the instrument was, it hurt like hell as it connected with his ribs.

Air flew out of his lungs as he grabbed the instrument and quickly realized a baseball bat might have felt better than the tire iron. He white-knuckled it, engaging in a game of tug-of-war with a guy half a foot shorter than Ian but built like a mac truck. The perp had on a ski mask and dark clothing. Not a professional hitman but not exactly someone who walked on the right side of the law. The details of his face were shielded.

Ian struggled to fill his lungs with air. The hit to the ribs had knocked the wind out of him. Once he had a handle on the tire iron, he yanked a couple of times. The perp jerked forward but held his ground. The next time Ian made a move to pull the tire iron toward him, he faked the guy out and let go instead.

Ski Mask flew backwards, landing hard on his backside. He brought his hands down to buffer his fall and Ian could have sworn he heard the guy's wrist snap when it hit the gravel drive.

Capitalizing on the moment, Ian dove straight at the intruder. He landed on top of him as the guy cursed and then engaged in a death roll. Gravel bit hard on Ian's skin where it was bare but he didn't have time to worry about the pain now. He'd pick the pieces out later. At this rate, it would take a while.

Ski Mask threw a knee into Ian's stomach. Now that just angered him even more. It also caused him to tighten into a ball to protect his vital organs. Instinct had a way of doing that.

"You won't get to her as long as I'm alive," Ian said, figuring he needed to anger the guy enough to make him talk. He reared his fist back before landing a hard blow to Ski Mask's cheekbone. Ian withdrew his hand and shook it. The pain he felt was nothing like what Ski Mask would be feeling right now.

Still, it stung like crazy and he'd been in enough fist-fights in his youth to realize this one was going to leave a few marks on him. The next thing he knew, he was being spun around again, the weapon in his hand went flying. He jerked out of the perp's grip and then scrambled to his knees. Crawling forward, he reached for his weapon stretching his body, arm, and fingertips only to end up yanked backward by a tight grip on his ankle.

Ian kicked as hard as he could, landing the tip of his boot on Ski Mask's nose. The man grunted and shouted to someone who must be nearby. The momentary freedom gave Ian the chance to scoot toward his gun. Mid-reach Ski Mask landed a body punch to Ian's kidneys that was going to leave a bruise. His hand was too close to give into the pain no matter how much instinct tried to force him to curl into a ball again.

As he felt the cool metal of the gun, Ski Mask hopped up to his feet. Just as Ian drew the weapon, the business end pointed toward Ski Mask, the guy bolted around the side of the U-Haul. Ian took aim at the perp's ankle and fired. The shot went wide but Ski Mask started hopping and zigzagging.

Ian sat up and barreled around the U-Haul in time to see a motorcycle had appeared in the distance. It didn't bother to stop. Ski Mask ran behind it until it slowed down enough for him to hop on. By now, the dust was so thick Ian was coughing.

He hurried toward the house. As he neared the front door, it swung open and Daphne stepped onto the porch, shotgun at the ready.

"Are you okay?" she asked, not checking him but aiming toward the dust cloud and keeping her focus there. She would be a fine tracker, he thought.

"I'm all right." He was frustrated more than anything else as he hopped onto the porch and ushered her inside. "Where's Henry?"

"In the bath," she stated.

"Still?" he asked.

"Yes," she confirmed.

"He didn't hear any of that?" he asked, seriously shocked. Then again, maybe the door was closed and the water running. Or he could think the noise came from the TV.

"Not to my knowledge," she stated.

"Good. Don't let him see me like this," Ian said as he locked the door behind them. "I'll clean up in the bathroom upstairs and call Sheriff Lawler. Keep Henry down here. Lawler will want to come out and conduct an investigation but I'd rather my son not see his father like this."

"Okay," Daphne said, and he could hear her voice tremble ever so slightly, despite the brave front she was putting up. She'd always been strong like that, even though she would need a minute to process once everything settled down. Her emotions always hit later. She'd always viewed it as a flaw, whereas he'd believed being calm in a crisis was one of her better gifts. "I'll put the shotgun away and then check on Henry."

She started toward the guest bedroom and then stopped. "They won't come back, will they?" she asked.

"Not tonight," he reassured. "The area is too hot. My guess is they will come in with a different approach next time. We can discuss it once I speak to the sheriff and you get Henry to bed."

Daphne nodded, some of the concern wrinkling her forehead seemed to ease. His comment appeared to offer some reassurance. She armed the alarm before disappearing into the bedroom as he took the stairs two at a clip. The downstairs was locked up tight so they should be good to go while he cleaned up his wounds. He had a first aid kit in his overnight bag that should help with the damage.

By the time he made it to the top of the stairs, he could tell his rib was probably fractured by the initial hit. Moving around was going to be a real pain. So was laughing. He grabbed supplies and headed into the bathroom, cursing the fact someone had gotten the upper hand on him as he made the call to the sheriff. Lawler's number was on speed dial after the past few months. Ian hadn't wanted to need it but there he was all the same.

HAD MOVING HERE BEEN the best of ideas?

Daphne walked to the bathroom door that was cracked open, shotgun at her side. She'd changed her mind about putting it away halfway to the bedroom. "Everything okay in there, buddy?"

"Yes, Mom," Henry said. He made a noise like he was an airplane crashing into a boat, his favorite pastime while he was in the shower.

"Five more minutes," she said. He always did better when she gave him a countdown. "Got it?"

"Okay," he stated but went right back to playing 'crash.'

This was one of those rare times she was actually glad that he'd been so consumed with playing that he hadn't heard any of what had gone down outside. She stood there for a long moment; grateful tonight hadn't turned into something much worse. She'd known it would only be a matter of time before her ex would figure out her location.

Daphne tucked the shotgun underneath her mattress after emptying it. She put the shells inside the top drawer of her dresser in a locked case and then walked around to each room on the first floor making sure the blinds were closed and curtains were pulled shut.

By the time she returned to the living room, Ian was on his way downstairs. He winced as he took each step no matter how much he tried to cover his pain.

"How bad is it?" she asked, realizing he wouldn't tell her the truth. Not that he was a liar but he would downplay his injuries, try to laugh them off as no big deal.

"Took a shot to the ribs that'll make it hard to laugh for a few days," he quipped with a forced smile. "Sheriff is on his way. He took my statement on the phone, but he wants to check the area while any tracks might be fresh. I asked him not to disturb the house if he didn't have to, because there's a little boy inside that I don't want checking over his shoulder every five minutes because he's living in fear."

"It'll be tough to explain why he can't go outside for a while," she said. He'd gotten a sunburn the day before. Maybe she could tell him she forgot to buy sunblock. He'd have to wait to go outside until she had time to run to the store. That might buy a day or two. What then?

"Those dogs were money well spent," Ian stated as he eased onto the sofa.

"Thank you," she said. "Mind if I sit with you?"

"Not at all." He started to scoot over but froze and winced.

"Can I get you anything, Ian? Water? Ibuprofen?" she asked, knowing full well he would go down the tough-guy route. It just seemed all kinds of wrong not to offer.

"Nope. I'm fine," he said without missing a beat.

This didn't seem like a good time to negotiate as he seemed to be taking stock in the damage.

"There are a couple of cuts that need doctoring. I'm going to have a humdinger of a bruise on my left side. But I covered the big scrapes," he said with a hint of pride. He'd seen to his wounds with care and she remembered how he'd been taught to do so while tracking dangerous poachers.

"You have so many scars," she said, trailing a finger along a two-incher on his shoulder.

"Good reminders, if you ask me," he countered. "With this one." He pointed to one that was half an inch round on his left forearm. "I learned not to run into a tree branch." He laughed.

"You're pretty banged up. Are you sure you're very good at what you do?" she teased, trying to lighten the mood in what had been a tense night.

"Poachers? Those are no problem. My family and the ranch are another story altogether but I'll improve," he said. "I'm just as determined to figure out how to pick up the pieces left by the Marshall and make it work. One involves my livelihood and the other involves my heart."

"I'd say both do," she countered. "There hasn't been a

time when you didn't love being a rancher, a Firebrand, and a loner."

Ian laughed. Winced.

"Not fair," he said.

"So, the only thing I have to do in order to torture you is make you laugh?" she teased.

"It would seem so," he quipped, holding onto his ribs. "I heard the other guy's wrist snap and I maybe clipped a piece of his ankle with a bullet."

Daphne involuntarily shivered. The thought of someone getting so close to the house—close enough to reach the front porch—caused her pulse to skyrocket. Having Ian here kept her nerves a notch below panic. As much as she wanted to hear every detail about what had just happened, she knew he had already given his side to the sheriff. Rather than pepper him with questions now, she decided to keep the conversation on him and the ranch.

"Has the poacher problem gotten worse?" she asked.

"It's about the same. I get into a few scrapes here and there," he said. "Not all of these scars come from fights."

"Where did the rest come from?" She frowned. It was difficult to think of her sweet and gentle Henry ever becoming as tough as his father.

"This one came from grilling." He pointed to a scar on his left hand.

"You're not supposed to cook yourself," she said, relieved for a break in tension. Now that she was home and felt secure for the first time in ages with Ian in the room, she couldn't imagine going back to the life she and Henry had been living on the run. The incident tonight took her back to a place she never wanted to go to again. One that she was scared and alone. At least with Ian here, someone had her back. For the first time in ten years, she could rely on someone else for a change. For the first time in a very long time, she felt hopeful.

Henry came out of the bath and into the living room, wearing his favorite dinosaur pajamas.

"You dried off and got dressed all by yourself?" Ian asked, sounding impressed.

"Yes, sir." Henry flashed eyes at Ian. "Mr. Ian, I mean." Henry shook his head, like he was shaking off a mistake. "Ian."

Daphne made a note to ask about that later.

"Did you brush your teeth?" she asked.

Henry shook his head again.

"Good. Because I saw ice cream being put in the freezer earlier, and a jar of hot fudge sitting on the counter. How about a before bed sugar rush?" Daphne hopped up off the couch to a nodding, smiling kiddo. "Last one to the kitchen does the dishes."

She took off before she finished her sentence and Henry darted right past her. She heard grunts and groans from the living room.

"Mind if I get in on a sundae?" Ian asked.

"As long as you're not too hurt to open and slice a couple of bananas," Daphne teased.

Henry's eyebrows knitted together as he watched Ian hobble into the kitchen.

"What happened, Ian?" Henry asked, wide-eyed.

"I had an accident in the yard a little while ago," Ian explained, moving beside Daphne where the bananas were. "If I was you, I'd listen to everything your mother tells you, or you might end up in as bad a shape as I am right now."

Henry nodded his agreement vigorously and Daphne smiled, appreciating the shout-out.

"Right now, your mother says you should take a seat at

the table and get ready for the best hot fudge sundae this side of the Pecos River," Daphne said, building on the moment and enjoying the three of them being in the same room, getting along like she'd seen in her mind's eye a hundred times over the past ten years.

She took a moment to stop and appreciate this moment happening to her little family, knowing that nothing lasted forever. She wanted to memorize this scene where Ian sliced bananas and she scooped ice cream while Henry sat anxiously at the table.

How would he react to learning Ian was his father? Would he be happy? Confused? Sad? They couldn't hold off on telling him forever. It didn't seem right or fair to him or Ian. She and Ian hadn't talked about the timing and as she saw the two of them taking tentative steps toward bonding it occurred to her that they shouldn't wait too long.

If Henry got to know Ian as a family friend, he might reject Ian as his father. Now that Ian was going to be Henry's life, it seemed important to tell him as soon as possible. But then she also didn't want her son to associate learning about his father with his sense of safety being ripped out from underneath him when Miles and his cousin struck again. And she was certain they were responsible.

When bowls were filled with a scoop of vanilla ice cream, Daphne settled at the table with Henry. Ian joined them a moment later.

"Mr. Ian," Henry said after taking his first bite of sundae.

"Yes," came the response.

"Do you know who your father is?" Henry's question caught Daphne off guard. She tried not to show her reaction to the question. Did Henry feel lacking in some way? Had she not done a good enough job with him? Guilt racked her for not mentioning Ian to Henry. Little did he know, he had an amazing Dad.

"I do," Ian responded. "Why do you ask?"

Henry shrugged. "Just curious."

"You're welcome to meet him someday if you'd like," Ian stated, seeming calm and collected. Based on the extra note of calm in his voice, he was freaking out about the question too.

"Nah. That's okay," Henry asked. "I just wondered if maybe you didn't have a father like me."

Ian opened his mouth to speak but seemed to think better of it as he clamped his lips shut. At this point, all Daphne could do was give Ian the look that said they would talk about this later. The look she got in response said there was no doubt in Ian's mind they would.

12

I an had to hold his tongue. He and Daphne would have a discussion soon about when the right time for the reveal was, but it needed to happen soon because he'd almost blurted it out. The only thing that had held him back, was the worry about adding to the stress and trauma Henry was already under with the move.

His cell buzzed as he finished the last bite of his ice cream. He glanced up at Daphne after checked the screen. "I'll be outside with Lawler." He purposely didn't mention the word *sheriff,* since most boys around Henry's age either wanted to be in law enforcement, work as firefighters, or be some version of a professional athlete.

"It's time to wind down for bed, buddy," Daphne said to a deflated Henry.

"Story time?" he asked, hopeful as Ian pushed up to standing.

"Help me with dishes first," Daphne stated.

At least Ian had won over the Dobermans. They followed Henry everywhere he went and were currently under the table at the boy's feet. Make no mistake about it, if

Ian did anything one of the dog's perceived as a threat his status would change instantly. The dogs were well trained to read moods.

Henry didn't whine. He picked up his bowl and walked it over to the sink with a smile that could melt the coldest heart.

"I'd like to move the U-Haul away from the front of the house," Ian said to Daphne. She grabbed her purse, dug around, and then tossed a pair of keys at him.

"Be my guest," she said.

"I imagine our guest will want to speak to you once you get Henry to bed," Ian stated.

She nodded.

"I won't be too long," she said. "In fact," she put her arm on Henry's shoulder, "change of plans. What do you think about taking your Game Boy to bed with you tonight instead of story time?"

"Yeah." Henry pumped his fists.

"I'll be out in a few minutes," Daphne said with a quick look of relief.

Ian pocketed the U-Haul keys figuring Sheriff Lawler would want to leave everything as it was outside until he finished his investigation. He greeted the sheriff on the porch.

Timothy Lawler had been two grades ahead of Adam in school, so that made Lawler forty years old. He and Adam knew of each other, considering Lawler had been a star quarterback who was being scouted by some big-name programs. A hit that broke his arm in four places ended his athletic prospects. Still, he'd managed to get off the game-winning throw and turned into quite a celebrity for the feat. The injury had ended his career and any hopes of playing college ball. He'd been one of those tall quarterbacks who could see the field and had a sixth sense about where his players were. As he told it, he'd gone to school and studied criminal justice instead and then followed in his father's footsteps in law enforcement. Based on height, he could easily fit in to the Firebrand fold. Height was where the similarities ended. Lawler was about as fair-skinned as they came, with ginger hair in a military cut, a hawk-like nose and compassionate brown eyes.

"Sorry for the late call," Ian said.

"No trouble at all. I was already out." Lawler had on his usual outfit of jeans, boots, and a tan shirt with the word 'Sheriff' embroidered on the right front pocket.

Ian gave the sheriff the rundown.

"Where did the fistfight take place?" Lawler asked after noting the basic description and location of injuries of the suspect.

"About here," Ian walked over to the front of the U-Haul and pointed. The lights he and Bronc had installed earlier in the day were doing their job, keeping the area well-lit at night.

Lawler illuminated the exact area with his camera flashlight before moving around to look at it from a few angles. He took pictures and collected several rocks as evidence.

"There's blood splatter on these," he explained before having Ian retrace his steps when he fired his weapon at the suspect and after placing several inside paper bags.

"I was on my side here," he pointed out the exact spot. His side imprint was etched into the gravel. He then showed the sheriff where his injuries occurred on his body. Bandages corroborated his story. Breathing hurt but his pride was injured even more at the fact the perp had gotten in the kicks and punches he had. Then, there was the tire iron, which had done the real damage to his ribs.

"Should I request a paramedic?" Sheriff Lawler asked after Ian described the blow he'd taken.

"Nah." Ian waved him off. "I'll be fine. Just a bruised rib or two."

"They could run an x-ray and fix you right up at the hospital," Lawler stated.

"I'm needed here and, besides, I've had worse happen to this body and healed up fine on my own." He would wrap his ribs after a shower. Compression should help ease some of the pain from movement.

"I know you're used to doctoring yourself up and further know that you can gauge how much pain you can take, so I won't press. I'll have to write in my report that you refused medical assistance," Lawler explained. "It's no big deal. Just didn't want you to have questions when you got a copy of the report and I'm required to notate these things when they come up."

"No offense taken," Ian stated.

After walking the sheriff through where the perp was running when Ian was almost certain he took at least a little skin from an ankle, Lawler thoroughly searched the area on his own. There was no sign of the tire iron. He bagged a few more rocks in individual paper bags.

"I have hope that the blood on these could lead us to the suspect. The rocks I collected by the front of the U-Haul could very well have your blood on them," Lawler continued.

Ian had expected that.

Daphne opened the front door and bounded out onto the porch. "Is this a good time for me to give my statement?"

"I think we're just about finished out here," Lawler stated. "Any chance we can come inside to hear the rest?"

"Can I offer you a cup of coffee?" Daphne offered.

"I'd like that a whole lot, Ms. Thompson," Lawler said. "Welcome home, by the way. Your father told me you'd be coming."

"Really? Was everything okay?" Concern lines creased her forehead.

"Yes. Sorry. Didn't mean to startle you. I ran into him at the post office the other day," Lawler explained.

Daphne smiled and then scanned the area before rubbing her arms and going back inside. Being out here seemed to affect her and Lawler probably picked up on it. At night, it was hard to see into the tree line. The house was about as secured as it could be without moving in a SEAL team. She had one of the best trackers in the country, Ian, which also meant he was better at finding the bad guys than holding up in a house like a sitting duck. There was no way he was leaving her and Henry alone even for a minute.

"While you head on inside, I'd like to move the U-Haul," Ian said. "It was parked too close to the house and made it easier for the jerk to surprise me."

"Understandable that you'd want to move it." Lawler nodded. "Are you planning to move the truck as well?"

"It was my intention," Ian stated.

"If you want to pitch the keys to me, I'll do it for you and then we can head inside together," Sheriff Lawler said.

"Here you go." Ian fished keys out of his pocket and tossed them over. The sheriff hadn't lost his abilities to catch. He snatched the keys out of thin air.

Ian climbed into the driver's seat of the U-Haul and closed the door as Lawler clicked the key fob to unlock Ian's truck.

Like a firework display on Fourth of July, the front of the truck exploded.

A BLAST OUTSIDE caused the tile floor to vibrate. Daphne dropped down onto all fours as she heard glass breaking in the living room. The security alarm blared. It was like time slowed to a standstill. Sound no longer existed. And the next few seconds happened all at once. Her first thought was Henry and her father, and her second was Ian and the sheriff in a very close second.

Before she could scramble into the living room, the back door burst open and a strong male figure picked her up from behind like she was a ragdoll that weighed nothing. Screaming did no good. She doubted anyone outside could hear after being in close proximity to a blast like that one. She did it anyway. There was no way she was going down easily.

Daphne screamed, kicked, and squirmed, trying to break free of the steel band around her torso as she was forcibly carried out the back door. With all the noise in front of the house, there was no way anyone heard her as she was forced into the woods and toward the southeast side of the property.

"You'll be sorry you ever left Miles, bitch," came the angry voice she knew all too well. "He gave you everything on a silver platter and you treated him like dirt."

"Leaving your cousin was the best day of my life," she ground out in between screams for help.

A hand came over her mouth but she bit down hard on it while continuing kicking like a wild banshee. The shotgun was still tucked inside her mattress. The shells were in the nightstand. Out here, she had no weapon and no way of defending herself.

"Where are you taking me?" she screamed.

"To a reunion," he said with a laugh that made her skin crawl. "You need to see what you've been missing out on before your eyes close for the last time. And that kid of yours will be next."

Panic gripped her. Her pulse climbed. Icy fingers gripped her spine. They had no reason to hurt Henry. She prayed they would leave her son alone. But she wouldn't give them the satisfaction of knowing how afraid she was.

"Hurt my child and you better sleep with one eye open for the rest of your life. Because he has a father and eight uncles who will not sleep until you're buried six feet under... still alive."

The threat caused an involuntary tremor to rock Cyrus. *Good.* It meant she was getting somewhere.

"Oh, that's right. Henry's father is back in his life and that's the reason we moved home. He knows everything, including who you are. The sheriff already turned in your names, so you'll be on every Wanted list in the state of Texas and beyond. There's no place left to hide," she continued, figuring screaming was doing no good anyway. Maybe she could keep working on Cyrus. "The Firebrands are one of the wealthiest families in the state. They're some of the best trackers in the country, so you'll never be able to lay your head down in the same place twice if anything happens to me or Henry. Mark my words when I say there is no length too far for them to go."

"You're bluffing," Cyrus said but she'd rattled him. He was doubling down on the tough-guy act, a sure sign of a growing insecurity.

"Am I?" she asked, finally gaining her confidence back. Miles might just kill her. But he needed to know what he'd be up against. Because she wasn't lying when she said the Firebrands wouldn't rest until Miles and his cousin were locked behind bars or six feet in the ground, and they wouldn't care which came first if anything happened to her or Henry. Ian would be especially angry if something happened to Henry's mother. She wished for more on the personal side with him but she also knew better than to be greedy.

"You never said Henry's biological father was a high-brow cattle rancher," Cyrus said. He paused for just a second, long enough for her to wiggle her right arm free and throw an elbow that knocked air from his lungs.

Cyrus grunted as he bent forward. She went flying to the ground, landing hard on dry earth. Sticks jabbed at her, poking her in the side and hands. Her hand went down hard too and she briefly felt it in her wrist. Not a good sign. If not for adrenaline, she feared she would be in serious pain right now.

Getting back to Henry in one piece was her sole priority. And Ian. The thought of never seeing him again slammed into her like a tornado, twisting up her insides and shredding everything in its path. Had she ever really stopped loving him?

Scrambling onto all fours, that vise-like grip wrapped around her stomach again. This time, she landed a foot to his ankle.

"Crazy bitch," he shouted after a spitting out a few more curses. Had she hit his bad ankle? Daphne slammed her heel at the same spot, connected.

Cyrus screamed out in pain. It made sense that he was the one who'd attacked Ian earlier. Cyrus must have stayed on property after the failed attempt to get past Ian. Either him or Miles must have tampered with the truck. It was clear they wanted Ian out of the picture and fast. Did they anticipate the sheriff being involved?

Daphne twisted and rolled but the vise grip around her midsection was unforgiving. A blunt object—a rock?—slammed against the back of her head. She managed to twirl enough to throw an elbow jab in Cyrus's face.

He spit off to the side. Blood?

She couldn't risk him taking control again or slamming the object into her skull once more, so she unleashed everything she had inside of her. Leaving nothing on the table, she wriggled, elbowed, kicked in a fury until the vise loosened.

A second later, she was crawling away from Cyrus. Pulling herself up using a tree trunk, she got her balance before taking off running. It was black as pitch outside. Even the moon was covered by the canopy of trees. She had no cell phone or flashlight to light the way. Hands out in front, feeling her way, she ignored the jabs of sharp twigs as she moved as fast as she could without slamming face first into a tree.

Then, a bright light shone from behind her and she could hear the sound of twigs snapping underneath heavy feet.

At least she had light now and could pick up the pace. Based on the sound of heavy footfall, Cyrus was nursing a bad ankle. But she could hear his heavy breathing and he was gaining on her.

Daphne bolted through the woods, her bare feet taking the brunt of the damage. Pain shot up her legs, making it hard to keep going. Painful stabs begged her to stop. *No way.* Not when there was a way out.

She knew this property like the back of her hand and there was only one chance of survival with Cyrus this close.

13

Ian's ears rang as he threw his shoulder into the door of the U-Haul and then bolted toward the sheriff's limp body on the ground near the truck. Everything slowed. Taking a knee, Ian immediately felt for a pulse. Got one. It was weak but he'd take it.

A quick assessment of the sheriff's visible injuries showed he had a piece of glass—windshield?—wedged in his left shoulder. There were too many arteries there for Ian to mess around with and he'd learned a long time ago to leave certain things alone.

The fastest way to get a cavalry on the scene would be the sheriff's radio. Since Lawler was unconscious, it wasn't like Ian could ask permission. He leaned over the sheriff's shoulder and pressed the walky-talky button.

"The sheriff is down. I repeat. The sheriff is down. Requesting all manner of emergency personnel to the Thompson residence immediately. Medical. Fire. Law enforcement. We need help. Now! Repeat. We need help," he said, unable to hear his own voice of the roar of the burning fire. Not that he would be able to hear anything over the ringing noise anyway.

He let go of the button and grabbed Lawler by the shoulders, needing to pull the sheriff away from the burning vehicle. Ian coughed as he chugged in the smokey air. All he could think about was dragging the sheriff to safety on the other side of the U-Haul and finding some clean air. His nose burned, and his vision blurred from all the smoke. Yes, breathing in the tainted air wasn't his biggest concern. It dawned on him that Daphne was nowhere to be seen. She would be out here by now if she could.

The second Lawler was on the other side of the U-Haul, Ian bolted to the front door. He saw the outline of his son at the front window and his gut clenched at the sight of the lonely figure. Daphne should either be with Henry, keeping him inside, or outside checking on the explosion. But windows had burst in the living room, and Daphne was nowhere to be seen. Henry could be standing on shards of glass; Ian gated toward the front door and ran inside.

"Watch your feet," Ian warned, hoping he wasn't yelling to be heard. The last thing he wanted to do was scare Henry or the dogs, who stood dutifully by his side, barking.

"Don't move. Okay?" he shouted over them.

Henry nodded.

"Cool fire," he said, clearly in shock and unable to grasp the gravity of the situation. Ian was thankful for small miracles and for the fact he could read lips. At least this incident might not scar Henry for life.

"It sure is, but we don't want to go near it," Ian confirmed as he stepped over glass to get to his son. At this point, Luna and Luis were baring their teeth. Ian shouted the command he'd heard Daphne give and prayed it would work.

The dogs quieted down immediately and a wave of relief

washed over him. With him being around recently and accepted by Daphne, the dogs seemed to accept him.

"Where is your mom?" he asked Henry.

"I don't know," Henry stated. His video game was still in his right hand and he had on button-up dinosaur pajamas.

Ian picked his son up as Mr. Thompson came down the stairs. His hair was soaked and he was half dressed, indicating he must have been in the shower.

"Where is Daphne?" Ian asked her dad.

"I have no idea," Mr. Thompson said with a shrug and wild eyes. "What happened?"

"I'll explain later. Right now, there's no time to waste and I need to ask a favor," Ian said.

Mr. Thompson's forehead creased as he nodded.

"Take Henry upstairs and lock both of you in your bedroom or bathroom, whichever has a sturdier lock," Ian stated. "Don't come out of your room until emergency personnel arrive. They're on the way now. The sheriff is out front 'sleeping' for the time being. Someone is on the way to help."

The nod from Mr. Thompson came quickly.

Ian walked Henry over to his grandfather, then handed him over.

"Fire extinguisher is in the kitchen pantry," Mr. Thompson instructed after taking Henry's hand.

"Thank you." Ian watched as the two hurried up the stairs, dogs on their heels. The second they were out of sight, he bolted to the pantry and retrieved the fire extinguisher. On the way in, he caught sight of the broken glass on the backdoor and the fact it had been left open.

Someone had been inside the house. Ian would bet money on Daphne's ex and his cousin. At least they had names. Names they'd given the sheriff. The jerks wouldn't get away with whatever it was they thought they could do to her.

Rage boiled inside his veins as he ran around the back of the house just in case he could see her. Hearing much of anything besides the ringing was a struggle.

The bomb had clearly been meant for him. These guys would now be facing attempted murder charges no matter what else happened. Folks with nothing to lose didn't exactly bring out the warm and fuzzies. He couldn't imagine trying to bring up Henry without Daphne. She was a rock. She'd been Henry's sole parent for the past nine and a half years.

And she would be in the future, he told himself. There was no other option. He would find her, and those bastards would pay.

Ian pulled the pin and then sprayed down the burning truck. There was just enough chemical to put out the blaze. He ran to Lawler's side next, tortured at the fact he was going to have to leave the sheriff here alone in his current state.

But he was losing time with whoever took Daphne. She had to have been taken. She would never leave her son alone and vulnerable. The question was where had she been taken to?

During the explosion, his ears had been blasted. Ian still couldn't hear right. Everything sounded like he was in a tunnel. At least the smoke was gone, and he was breathing in clean air again.

Assessing the situation, the perp must have come in through the backdoor. The activity in front had to have been a distraction. Had someone been waiting in the woods for the explosion? Or was that meant to take Ian out, so getting to Daphne would be easier prey?

Any evidence like fingerprints would have been blown up with the explosion. Fire would have destroyed what was left.

Ian glanced around, figured the only way to get to the backdoor without risk of being seen was through the woods in back of the house. He bolted around the corner and searched the surrounding area. His eyes had already adjusted to the dark, so seeing wasn't a problem. The ringing noise was driving him insane though.

Leaving the sheriff on the ground, vulnerable, was a stab to his gut, but he didn't have any choice. He needed to find Daphne.

The distant sounds of sirens splitting the air gave some relief from Ian's guilt at running in the opposite direction.

To the back of the house was a field before the tree line. He'd spent plenty of hours chasing Daphne through this area and beyond in their youth. The memories, good memories, came crashing down around him.

It also occurred to him that he'd just let her disappear out of his life. He'd been blaming her all these years for walking away but he'd been too busy licking wounds to go after her. And he could have.

She'd made it difficult, but Ian also realized when he really put his mind to something, it got done. It was a Firebrand family trait that had been handed down from generation to generation. Ian was beginning to see his responsibility here. How had he been such an idiot to only blame her?

They'd been kids and had both suffered. Blaming her for his actions, especially after learning the Marshall's part in all this, was as immature as they came.

Ian stopped at the tree line and listened for any sign of Daphne, a yell for help or an engine. ATV? Motorcycle?

There was nothing, but then his hearing wasn't exactly reliable right now. Frustration was a gut punch.

One thing was certain. Ian couldn't lose Daphne a second time. He wouldn't survive it.

Since standing here and doing nothing wasn't an option, he took a risk and darted inside the trees, using his cell phone to light the way.

DAPHNE'S FEET, slick with blood, struggled for purchase on the tree dotted hill. Cyrus was so close she could hear him panting for air behind her on the steep incline. She risked a backward glance to see how much distance she had. The mistake cost her as his fingers wrapped around her ankle.

He yanked her onto her backside, and then they were both rolling down the hill. Tree stumps nailed her as she tried to grab onto a limb strong enough to stop her. Just over the hill was her safe place. The destination was so close. She couldn't lose it this close.

Grasping at anything, she grabbed fistfuls of dirt and rock. Finally, her hand made contact with a branch sturdy enough to hold her weight. She held onto it for dear life before she stopped. Her arm felt like one of those bungy cords, extending until it looked like it might snap before bouncing back.

Nothing mattered except getting to her safe place so she could get away from Cyrus. He was stronger than he looked and she'd realized she was no match for him punch for punch. She had a secret weapon, though, if she could just get to it.

Daphne screamed for help even though no one out here would hear her. She scrambled to her feet and started back up the hill, clawing and digging her fingernails into the hard ground to get there faster.

For some reason, Cyrus didn't seem to be following her. She couldn't risk looking back at him. She could only pray he was knocked out and that was the reason she didn't hear him breathing or the sound of twigs.

And then she heard a motor in the distance, getting louder. A motorcycle or ATV. She couldn't pinpoint the sound and had no plans to stick around to find out. A scary thought struck. Was that the reason Cyrus was being quiet?

Her pulse raced and her heart battered the inside of her ribcage as she made progress on the hill. The soles of her feet felt like they'd been through the shredder and she could already tell they were swelling. But there was no time to stop and do anything about it, so she kept pushing as the motor became louder.

It worried her that Cyrus had stopped. It meant his backup was on the way. It meant she was about to be outnumbered.

At the midway point of the hill, the engine came to a stop. A few feet of progress later, she heard a voice that made her blood run ice cold. *Miles.* She should have known it was only a matter of time before he joined the party.

"You can run all you want, Daphne. There's no one else around," he shouted up to her. "Cyrus is already making his way to the other side of the hill. You're trapped. So, go ahead and wear yourself out. That's all you're doing, by the way. We got you and there's nowhere else to go."

Miles didn't know this area like she did. And Cyrus was about to get a big surprise if he made it over to the other side of the hill. She would get there first because she was taking the fastest route and she would watch while he got what was coming to him.

Miles might be right. They might get hold of her and destroy her. But she wasn't going down without a fight, and she had a whole lot of fight left inside her.

The thought of never seeing her boy again fueled her to keep going. And Ian. He was right there in her thoughts alongside Henry. It just seemed wrong they were robbed of their chance to be a family all those years ago. And now? They'd just gotten back in the same room with each other. They were discussing co-parenting. The Marshall might be gone but his damage had been done.

If she died, the Marshall won. Miles won. Cyrus won.

Daphne couldn't allow it.

IAN HEARD the unmistakable sound of a motorcycle engine, out in the middle of nowhere and at night. He redirected his body, changing course to the sound. The fact it stopped suddenly made no sense. Unless there was a chase, and the trees became too thick to navigate. Or...

With a sharp intake of air, he realized exactly where Daphne would be headed. A motorcycle wouldn't be able to get there. He'd tried on horseback, but the hill was too steep. If she was heading to the apiary, or bee farm in laymen's terms, the motorcycle couldn't follow.

It was time to turn up the gas. Ian pushed his legs harder and pumped his arms. And then he heard Daphne's cry for help.

There was at least one person, possibly others. Two? More? It could be Miles and Cyrus. The motorcycle wouldn't have made it through the thicket surrounding the back of the yard near the house, so that meant there had to be two.

Ian slowed down as he neared the hill that led to the apiary. And then he heard the sound of a swarm of bees. More shouting had him increasing the speed again. He moved to the more difficult terrain where no one would expect a person to be. He pulled his weapon from his ankle holster, thankful he'd thought to leave it on earlier and climbed the steeper part of the hill.

Coming in from this angle would give him more protection from bullets being fired and would offer more of a barrier. He could climb down the other side while being shielded by the trees. It would take a few minutes longer. Minutes he wasn't certain he had.

A cloud of bees swirled overhead. The nest had been stirred up, angered. As he made it halfway down the other side of the hill, a figure methodically made its way toward him. Daphne?

He wouldn't take a risk. Instead, he positioned himself behind a tree and aimed the business end of his gun at the person moving.

14

D aphne kept a low profile as she climbed toward safety. The bees were out and buzzing. She'd been stung three times already. But Miles was allergic, so he couldn't risk sticking around.

As she made her way methodically up the hill, an arm reached out from behind a tree and grabbed her. In the next second, a hand clamped over her mouth but before she could bite down, hard, she recognized a familiar citrusy scent as she was hauled against a muscled chest. Ian.

"Be quiet, Daphne. It's me," Ian's voice washed over her and through her. She couldn't imagine a better sound than his deep timbre as the first real hope she would make it out of these woods alive struck. This seemed like a good time to remind herself they weren't to safety yet.

He removed his hand from her mouth and replaced it with a tender kiss.

"Let's get out of here," he whispered before clasping their fingers and making the trek back up the hill.

"There's two of them and Miles is allergic to bees," she said low. "I have no idea about Cyrus."

"He'll protect his cousin, no doubt," he said as they crested.

There was no sign of the motorcycle engine firing up and Daphne wasn't sure if that was a good or bad thing. Climbing down, her feet started screaming at her. Adrenaline seemed to be fading. Being here with Ian made it all bearable. Her heart squeezed at the thought the two of them could work together to bring up Henry. She hadn't allowed herself a moment to live in a world where the three of them were a family. Families came in all shapes and sizes. The possibility of Henry having his father in his life for the long haul nearly brought tears to her eyes. She'd shoved the hope down so deep that ten years later, as it began to surface, she wondered if she could trust it. Because hope could be a very cruel thing, she'd learned the hard way. It could leave her lying awake every night wondering 'what if' and going over the 'maybes' until she couldn't think straight any longer.

Daphne had had far too many sleepless nights, especially in the early years; the pain of walking away from Ian and shutting her best friend out of her life when she'd needed him the most had nearly crippled her.

Granted, she was older now and much stronger. Wiser, she hoped. Being with Ian after all these years still felt like the most natural thing. Like the world finally righted itself and she was exactly where she was supposed to be. No more longing. No more waiting. No more wishful thinking.

Could she ever forgive the Marshall for interfering? For taking away the one person she'd ever loved? *Still loved?*

What choice did she have? He was gone now. His legacy with his family wasn't something she would wish on any person. He left this world unloved and she couldn't think of a worse fate.

So, she would find a way to forgive him and let go of the anger she'd been holding onto for all these wasted years.

A dark thought occurred to her. What if being together caused her and Ian to be killed? Who would care for Henry then? Both of his parents would be gone. Her father would be too frail to care for her son. Did the Firebrands know Henry was one of them? His last name was Thompson.

If they did, she knew one hundred percent her son would be welcomed into the family and well cared for. Did she want to consider the possibility of a world where he grew up without her? No. Practically speaking, she might not get out of these woods alive. An idea popped.

"Do you think we should split up?" she asked Ian as they made to the midway down point.

"I'm not losing you again, Daphne," he said with the kind of resolve that sent an electrical current rippling through her.

"What about Henry?" she asked. "If something happened to us both...where would that leave him?"

Ian lifted her hand and kissed the back of it.

"We're not going anywhere," he stated. "Nothing is happening to you on my watch. Understand?"

"You can't guarantee that," she said, as much as she wanted it to be true. "There are no guarantees in life. I think we've both learned that."

"No. But there are choices," he said low and under his breath. "I, for one, am choosing to live through this because Henry is worth it. You're worth it. And what we have is worth it."

She had no idea what all he was covering in that statement but she sure liked the way it sounded.

"I'm not giving up, if that's what you think," she defended. "Henry needs two parents, but he won't survive without one of us. My father can't take care of himself let alone a nine-year-old."

"Stick by my side, Daphne. I promise to get you out of this alive. But just in case, my brother Grayson already knows about Henry and, either way, Henry has a huge family waiting for him. We just need to live through this so we get to see the look on his face when he realizes it," Ian said. There was something about the resolve in his voice that made a believer out of her too.

Being practical held no bearing any longer. She leaned into the feeling of being protected. Daphne had never needed anyone in her life and she could still get by on her own. She'd done a great job with Henry so far, considering he was literally the best kid ever in her very biased opinion. Having someone to lean on for a change was nice. She would lean into it, if only for a few a little while.

As they made it to the bottom of the hill, Ian bolted toward the house. He had to be wondering the same thing as her. Was there a third person involved? Had they made it to the house first?

"What happened at my dad's? I heard an explosion and then I was snatched from the kitchen before I could do anything," Daphne said, panting as she tried to keep up. Her feet screaming against movement but a fresh boost of adrenaline keeping the pain at bay temporarily.

"The sheriff was injured in the blast," Ian said as he pulled her into a dead run. "I called for help and sent Henry with your father and the dogs into a locked upstairs room."

Daphne's legs burned and her lungs clawed for air. But it was her feet that finally caused her to trip and nearly faceplant.

"What is it?" Ian immediately stopped. The link between them was the only thing that had kept her upright.

"No shoes," she said, sitting up and picking a rock out of the pad of her left foot.

Ian muttered a curse.

"I didn't know. I'm sorry I made you run." With that, he scooped her up and started jogging. Carrying her presented a challenge in the thickest part of the woods but at least they'd outrun the bees. She'd taken a couple of stingers, but it was nothing she hadn't survived before. She and Ian both had taken their fair share over the years, playing a little too close.

Out of nowhere, a light shined at their eyes. Daphne's eyes closed out of instinct but she forced them open to a squint. Ian stopped running and positioned them behind a tree that blocked part of the light.

A shot fired, pinging the tree not an inch away from her head.

"Can you stand up?" Ian asked.

"Yes, of course," she said as he set her down then tucked her behind him.

He drew his weapon, aimed at the source of the blinding light, and fired. Then, he urged them to move to a new spot a few feet over. Daphne's worst fears were being realized. One of them had a better chance of survival if they split up. Ian would never agree so she had to take matters into her own hands.

As he prepared to fire the next shot, she back peddled a few steps. The second he fired, she bolted. She could only pray he would understand and forgive her if anything happened. She couldn't risk both of Henry's parents being killed and this gave them a fighting chance for one of them to survive.

∼

I<small>AN</small> <small>GLANCED</small> <small>AROUND</small> as he reached for Daphne, realizing she was gone. He bit back a curse. Her comments earlier about splitting up made sense—he knew that on some level —but there was nothing inside him that could make the decision to part ways again. He couldn't do it. Wouldn't apologize for it either. They'd lost too many years and he didn't want to spend another second without his best friend by his side.

The crack of a bullet split the air as he put his back against a tree. The shot fired wide and a few feet away, near where he'd last been standing and he'd heard it through the ringing in his ears. At least some of his hearing was starting to come back. The threat to Daphne and Henry was so close Ian could almost reach out and touch it. He was torn between staying put and dealing with the threat while he had it within reach or going after Daphne while she was still close enough to find.

Eliminate the threat, and he would eradicate the reason to run in the first place. But there could be two folks out there. They might have split up the same as him and Daphne seemed to be doing.

Ian released a string of curses under his breath. As far as no-win situations went, this one was a doozy. Since he couldn't hear the sound of twigs snapping, which would give him a general direction, Daphne could be anywhere. Going after her could cause more damage than good.

With a sharp sigh, Ian fired a shot to distract whoever was near. It had to be Miles or his cousin Cyrus, based on what Daphne had said a few minutes ago. After firing, Ian crouched down low and duckwalked to a tree several feet in the opposite direction. He popped up and fired to give the impression he was moving east. He immediately crouched and backtracked past his original location.

On his own, he could move stealthily and quickly. Two of his biggest assets in the years he'd been tracking poachers.

Ian continued west, making a wide circle. Several shots were fired in the opposite direction, so he closed in from behind until he was close enough to get a visual on the target. When he moved, he limped. This was the jerk who'd attacked Ian. And he was alone.

At this range, Ian could put a bullet in the man's back but since there was no honor in that, and dying was too easy a way out, Ian crept up from behind instead. Slowly, steadily, methodically, he moved until he was within striking distance of the bastard.

In one swift motion, Ian threw himself forward and wrapped his left arm around the perp's neck, placing him in a chokehold. With his free right hand, he swiped the gun from the perp's hand.

"Remember me?" Ian bit out in the perp's ear. "Payback is going to be hell."

The perp grabbed at Ian's arm. His strength was surprising but he was no match for Ian. All he had to do was think about all the years he'd been without his son and enough rage filled him to squeeze harder.

The perp tried to kick but Ian was prepared for it. Size-wise, the guy was no match. So, it was a matter of holding on until the perp passed out in a few more seconds as he was temporarily deprived of oxygen.

The perp dug his fingers into Ian's forearm to no avail.

"You're going to rot in jail, so you can spend every long day thinking about how you ruined people's lives," Ian said moments before the perp's body went limp.

Ian let the perp fall. His body landed hard on the dry, cracked earth. Momentarily out of breath, Ian panted to get air in his own lungs again. The fight had drained his energy and his own physical wounds were threatening to bring him to his knees. He had no cell and no way to connect with Daphne. Since he'd left her family home in a flurry, he had no rope with which to tie the perp's arms behind his back.

He might have been able to carry Daphne but adrenaline was fading and he might just have to sit on this perp until daylight or someone showed up.

Law enforcement would look for him and Daphne. The woods would be an obvious place to start and, hopefully, someone would think of checking the bees. If not tonight, then the beekeeper would be here in the morning. His own cell was lost somewhere in the woods.

Ian could hold on until then, despite how badly his body cried out in pain. He would literally sit on top of this jerk until someone came within shouting distance. He'd shout now, but there was one other person lurking in these woods.

In fact, Ian took his belt off before turning the perp face down in the dirt. He positioned the perp's head so he could breathe before belting his hands behind his back. It would do for now, but if the guy put up much of a fight he would most likely be able to wriggle out of the makeshift cuffs.

The next thing Ian did was locate the perp's weapon. It wasn't hard to find since he knew which direction to search. He checked the clip to assess ammunition and then patted down the perp in case there were other hidden weapons. The clip had three bullets left. There didn't seem to be any others on the perp.

Next, Ian fished the man's wallet out of his back pocket. He picked up the cell phone the perp had been using to blind Ian and checked his identity. Cyrus Nolan. Miles's cousin. That meant Miles was out here somewhere. Possibly others but Ian had a feeling it was just the two of them on this mission.

They were clearly bent on revenge, especially considering Daphne had left Miles two years ago and he still came after her every chance he got. The charges against Cyrus were racking up too. Attempted capital murder would be the one to put him away for the rest of his life. The other crimes would add multiple life sentences and guarantee there was no chance of parole.

The flashlight feature was still on, so Ian picked up the man's cell phone. Was there any way he could use it without knowing the password? Everyone password protected their phone now. Thumbprint? Would that work?

Ian pressed the cell to Cyrus's thumb and the screen lit up. He had no phone numbers memorized but he could call 911.

He quickly realized the problem there. No service. It was a common problem out on ranch land and he couldn't remember where at the Thompson's had coverage. It had been too long to recall all the dead spots except to say there were many.

Hope that Daphne would return to this area, now that the bullets had stopped, sparked inside him. Or would she be afraid something had happened to him and it wasn't safe to come back?

And besides, with Miles still out there, she really wasn't safe. A twig snapping to Ian's right sent his pulse skyrocketing.

15

The quiet was eerie.

Daphne stayed crouched low, afraid to move out of her safe spot midway in between the house and the hill. It was black as pitch outside even though her eyes had adjusted to the darkness. Her feet screamed with pain and she doubted she could walk on them if she tried.

A noise to her right sent her pulse racing. She had no idea where Ian was or who had been back there in the gun battle. Cyrus and Miles were wandering around here somewhere and she could only pray Ian had survived.

He was one of the best trackers in the state, if not the country. Having to watch her had done nothing but slow him down. Leaving had given him a shot at not only survival but being proactive in taking down the shooter.

Sticking around was dangerous for them both. Even though she was second-guessing herself like crazy, she was convinced she'd done the right thing by taking off. There was no way she could help him fight and she was being the worst possible hinderance. Ian's survival skills were topnotch and he would find a way to live—*if* he wasn't being distracted by trying to save her.

Together, they'd gotten away from the hill. He had a fighting chance to take down the shooter.

Daphne sighed. The thought of losing Ian again when she'd only just found him nearly gutted her. She hadn't stopped thinking about him in the ten years they'd been apart. The notion that her actions could cause his death nearly sent her over the edge of despair.

All she had to keep her going right now was her strength —strength that had gotten her through some difficult patches in the road. She needed to pull on what was left of it to remind herself Ian was the best at what he did.

She'd survived so far. If she could get through the night alive, she'd be fine. Thoughts of reuniting with Henry kept her from hitting rock bottom. Thoughts of the three of them together as a family kept her from hollowing out. Thoughts of finding Ian on the other side of this mess kept her from giving in to the darkness trying to suck her under.

Daphne quieted her mind by focusing on breathing. It was a simple thing, really. She did it all day and night without much consideration. And yet breathing was one of the most powerful things. It brought oxygen to her cells and carried the bad stuff out, cleansing her. *Breathe.*

Another sound caused her to still.

A twig?

A wild animal?

Help?

Or was it Miles or Cyrus stalking her, unwilling to give up even after all this time? Miles had threatened her before she'd packed up an overnight bag and Henry's favorite teddy bear. They'd left with nothing two years ago and everything at the same time. She'd learned quickly that possessions meant nothing in a loveless house. She'd learned the most important thing was having Henry with her, safe and sound. And she'd learned it wasn't difficult to leave everything behind when she knew she was gaining her life back.

Miles didn't get to take that away.

Daphne felt around on the ground for something sharp to use as a weapon. Her fingers smoothed over a pointed rock. She closed her hand around it and brought it to her lap. Next, she located a stick that was strong enough to poke someone's eyes out.

If Miles or Cyrus showed, she'd be ready for them.

Minutes passed without any movement around her. Then, what had to have been an hour went by with still nothing. Adrenaline had long ago worn off and exhaustion set in. Daphne figured she could close her eyes for a few minutes and try to refill the well. She closed her eyes and, before she knew it, fell asleep.

The crunch of heavy boots on twigs shocked her awake. It was still dark outside and she was still in a sleep fog that left her disoriented. Blinking her eyes a few times, she strained to get a look at whatever was moving nearby.

Daphne hugged her knees to her chest. All she could hear was the sweet sound of Henry's voice in her head, filling her with resolve. Then, there was Ian to think about. Would life be so cruel as to take him away again when they'd only just found each other?

She listened for any sign this could be him. Was there any way he would clomp through the woods, making his presence so obvious? It wasn't likely.

Miles or Cyrus might not be so intelligent. Then again, they'd pulled off putting an explosive on Ian's truck and also managed to snatch her from her father's kitchen. Miles had most likely been plotting against her from the day she left. He could have been keeping an eye on her father's place in the event she came home.

The heavy footsteps seemed to be heading right toward her and now there was an occasional flash of light. There was no way the person walking toward her was Ian.

"OVER HERE," Ian said when he heard the squawk of a deputy's radio nearby. "My name is Ian Firebrand. I'm sitting on the person responsible for Sheriff Lawler's injuries."

Deputy Lynn Ramirez stepped into view. "I know what happened. I heard your voice on the radio earlier and I've been looking for you ever since."

"What about Daphne Thompson?" he asked. "Has she been found?"

"I'm sorry. We're still looking for her," Deputy Ramirez said as she walked over. "What do we have here?"

"Cyrus Nolan," Ian informed. "He's related to Miles Nolan. The two are cousins. I'm one hundred percent certain this is the guy who jumped me earlier, right before my vehicle blew up. Daphne said he broke into the kitchen and carried her out the back door during all the chaos."

Ramirez gave him a hand up before dropping a knee in Cyrus's back. A minute later, she handed over Ian's belt having replaced it with proper handcuffs. "How long has he been unconscious?"

"He's been in and out," Ian said. "Every time he woke up, he thought he wanted to fight me, so I knocked him out again. I can't promise he doesn't have a concussion, but he's alive and should be fit to stand trial."

Ramirez's smirk said it all as she called in their location over the radio.

"Miles may not have left the hives where the bees are kept over the hill," Ian said.

"Mr. Thompson said to look there for the two of you," Ramirez informed.

Ian nodded.

"I have to look for her," he said.

"There's still a perp on the loose," Ramirez stated. "And you're not looking in great shape here. Why not stick around and let us do our job? I can have a medic to you in a matter of minutes."

"She's out here somewhere," he said, unable to accept the fact Miles might have found Daphne first. "I have to go."

Ramirez gave him a look like she understood. "I'll hold down the fort here. You can finish giving your statement after you find her."

"Thank you," he stated.

"Good luck," she said. He hoped he wouldn't need it.

Ian took off in the direction she'd headed. It would have taken her east of the hill and maybe too far around to the other side. She wouldn't go back to the hill. He stopped in his tracks. Years of honed instincts told him she would make her way back to Henry. The fact she hadn't made it caused anger to boil through his veins.

Turning back, he took the route they'd taken a hundred times over the years. Stealthily, he moved toward the Thompson home. Muscle memory directed his movement at this point. His body ached with every forward step but he had to find her. If there was even a slight chance Daphne was out there alive and needing his help, he would keep going.

Halfway in between the hill and the family home, he

stopped at seeing slight movement out of the corner of his eye. Since it could be Miles, Ian investigated without making so much as a peep.

The minute he realized it was her, he whispered, "I'm here."

"Ian?" the quiet voice responded. *Her* voice.

It was the sweetest sound he'd ever heard and he realized in that moment he never wanted to be apart from her again. Not for one second. Not if he didn't have to be.

Daphne crawled out from behind a tree and he remembered her feet were damaged from running in the woods with no shoes.

"How bad is it?" he asked, dropping down to her level and pulling her into an embrace.

"I doubt I can walk, and I know you can't carry me," she said, looping her arms around his neck.

They kissed, sweet and tender.

"I can't believe you're okay," she said after pulling back from the kiss.

"I'm a little banged up, but I got Cyrus," he said. "A deputy has him in handcuffs as we speak."

"What about Miles?" she asked.

"No one has seen him," he said, feeling her heart race with the news. "Which doesn't mean anything yet."

"There was no motorcycle engine," she stated. "I've been listening for it."

"I have too, and I believe we're thinking the same thing," he admitted.

"The bees," she said.

He nodded.

"I have to get you out of here," he started. "But I want you to know that once you're safe again, I'd like to talk."

"I've been thinking too," she stated as a noise stopped them both.

The sound of heavy boots and twigs breaking came with a flashlight and the glorious squawk of a deputy's radio.

"Over here," Ian stated. "Ian Firebrand and Daphne Thompson are over here."

A deputy came running over. He was a new hire that Ian hadn't met yet. He shined a light in the area, careful not to hit them directly in the eyes.

"Mr. Firebrand and Ms. Thompson?" he asked, looking like he was registering the details of their faces.

"Yes, sir," Ian responded.

"Deputy Ramirez put out a message for us to drop everything we were doing and find the two of you," he said. "She wanted me to relay a message."

Ian nodded.

"They found Miles Nolan in the bees, just like you thought they would. The threat is gone," he stated. "I'm supposed to radio for help and get the two of you anything you need."

Daphne tucked her chin to her chest, like she did when she was trying to hide the fact she was crying. "We're safe."

"Yes, ma'am," the deputy said. "Please excuse me while I call it in." He spoke into the radio and then the sounds of cheers came through. "Everyone appreciates how you saved Sheriff Lawler's life."

"Henry and Mr. Thompson?" Ian asked.

"They're waiting for your return at the house, I'm told," the deputy said before quietly giving their location through the radio but Ian no longer cared.

He turned to Daphne, bringing his hand up to her beautiful face.

"We've lost so much time together when all I ever

wanted to do was get old enough to marry you and build a family. I've dated so many people and none could ever measure up to the perfection that is you," he said.

Tears streamed down her cheeks. He thumbed one away.

"I love you, Daphne," he continued. "I've been in love with you my whole life and I know it's the real deal. I don't have any questions as to whether or not it can last or if the time is right. Because I've been waiting for this day and didn't even realize it. I've come up with a million excuses as to why one person or the other wasn't the 'one' when there was only ever one explanation...they weren't *you*."

"I love you, Ian. I always have and I always will," Daphne said by way of response.

"Then make me the happiest person on earth and say you'll marry me." He was already on one knee, so he took her hand in his. "I don't have a ring but you can have anything you want if you'll say yes."

"Ian Firebrand. You are so many things to me. Best friend. First love. Only love. The only thing I've learned in the past ten years is how awful life can be without you. So, yes, I'll marry you. I love you with all my heart and soul, and I can't wait to become an official family," she said.

Ian kissed his bride-to-be, his best friend, his home.

"I'd like to be the one to tell Henry that I'm his father. I'd like him to know we're going to be a family," he said against Daphne's lips when they stopped kissing. "And I'll do everything I can to ensure your father gets the best medical care possible. You're not alone anymore, Daphne. I'm here too. Whatever life brings."

"Together. You and me with Henry," she said a little breathy, like she was finally exhaling air that she'd been holding in far too long. "That's all I've ever wanted."

~

THE JOURNEY back to the house went by fast as Ian walked toward his future, his son. The marriage proposal didn't feel complete without Henry being part of it. Henry was in the backyard, distracted with Luna and Luis when Ian and Daphne broke through the trees. Daphne had received medical attention and was given a pair of shoes from a deputy who'd volunteered to give hers up so she could make the trek home.

The second their little boy saw his mother, he bolted toward her. The Dobermans kept pace as Mr. Thompson sat down, like he'd been on alert praying for this moment to happen and fearing it wouldn't.

"Momma," Henry shouted, a mix of joy and relief packed inside that one word.

The trio plus dogs met in the middle of the yard after Daphne leaned into Ian and picked up the pace. She sat down as Henry dove toward them. Ian caught the young boy in time to soften the impact of landing in his mother's waiting arms. Seeing the two of them together and knowing the three of them were going to be a forever family was almost enough to bring Ian to his knees. His heart filled with love and his eyes leaked.

The Dobermans got in on the action, licking Daphne's face as though they realized the weight of this homecoming. All Ian could do was smile, ear-to-ear. His life hadn't felt complete since Daphne left town. There'd been a hole in his chest the size of a clear Texas night sky. His world had tipped on its axis and never felt the same.

Now, with the three of them, dogs he didn't even know he wanted, and Mr. Thompson, the world righted itself again.

Ian sat next to Daphne with his legs criss-crossed. Henry settled in his mother's lap as he beamed up at Ian.

"Hey, little man, I have something to ask you," Ian started, searching for the right words.

"What's that?" Henry perked up.

"I wanted to know if it would be okay with you if your mom and I got married," Ian said. It was a strange dynamic to feel so nervous about the approval of a nine-year-old.

Henry's gaze widened before bouncing to meet his mother's eyes.

She smiled and nodded.

"I know how much you like Ian and he wants the three of us to be a family," she said. Ian could tell she was slightly nervous too.

"Would it be forever?" Henry asked.

"I promise to love your mother for the rest of my life," Ian said, taking the lead. "And I'll love you too, Henry. With all my heart."

Henry's face lit up, causing a few more tears to leak out of Ian's eyes.

"Would you be my dad?" Henry asked, sounding hopeful.

This felt like the exact right time to deliver the news. Ian glanced at Daphne, checking to see if it was okay. The warm smile she gave in return was all the answer he needed.

"I *am* your dad, Henry. I didn't know it until you came to your grandfather's house to live, and that's why I haven't been around, but that changes now," Ian said.

Henry wiggled out of his mom's lap. His tiny arms wrapped around Ian's neck in a hug that threatened to turn Ian into a water faucet.

"My mom always told me that my dad was the best person in the whole world and that he would love me to the moon and back as soon as he met me," Henry said with excitement. Then came, "I hoped it was going to be *you*."

Two words described Ian's response to his son...*water works*.

"You've met me now, Henry. And I promise to be here for you every day for the rest of my life," Ian managed to get out as Daphne's fingers wound their way through his. She managed to join in the hug.

In this moment, Ian's world was finally right again.

Hudson Firebrand was still chewing on the news his little brother was getting married. *And then there was one. The cheese stands alone.* Not only was Hudson the last single person on his side of the family left single, but his baby brother beat him to the punch. If that wasn't enough to digest, Ian was already a father. *A father.*

What was happening in the world?

Hudson shook his head. If someone had told him last May that by fall all eight of his brothers would be married or planning a wedding, he would have asked them what well they'd been drinking from. Now? All he could do was shake his head and laugh. Or cry. It all depended on the day.

Speaking of water, the joke there must be something in it was becoming a little too real. *Note to self: stop drinking water.*

The early morning October breeze gave no hint of relief from the scorching hot summer. There was not a drop of rain in sight. The two-year drought was taking its toll on these parts.

Hudson dismounted Honey, his mare. He tied her reins to a nearby tree before cresting Crater Rock. There was something about staring down his thirtieth birthday that left him with an unsettled feeling. Like there was something he was supposed to do and wasn't. Or something he should be trying to achieve. He'd been planning to talk to the family about it, but the feeling it was time to move on had taken hold. After saving almost all of his money for most of his life and deciding to let his family buy him out of his part of the inheritance, he'd decided to move to Austin and put down money on a lease. The time for Hudson Tacos to take flight had come. Now, he just needed to break the news to the family. With all the changes since the Marshall died, he wasn't sure how his brothers would take the news. His parents seemed to be in their own bubble since his father's stroke. His father seemed to be trying to make amends after a lifetime of mistakes.

All the recent changes had spurred Hudson into thinking about his own future and wondering if he was chasing his dreams or doing what was expected of him. He loved the land. He loved his family. He loved Lone Star Pass. What he couldn't figure out was why he felt like something was missing in his life, something big.

In no way, shape, or form was he ready to get married. The idea of kids made him want to loosen his collar. It was probably all the weddings and marriage talk that was getting inside his head, making him think he should be at a different point in life. *Tacos,* he thought. Now, he just needed to call a family meeting and drop the news. His cousin Vaughn's recent phone call had stopped Hudson from setting it up. He wanted to know why his cousin was calling out of the blue.

Hudson and Vaughn had been in the same grade, most

of the same classes, and on the same sports teams. Hudson had been closer to Vaughn than his own brothers, so he felt like a real jerk for not reaching out after Vaughn's mother was arrested for attempted murder recently. The subject didn't come up during the call either. All Vaughn had said was that he couldn't talk long. Then, he requested the two of them meet at Crater Rock. Hudson had agreed to the meet-up, Vaughn had ended the call, and now Hudson was here, waiting for his cousin to show.

Crater Rock had been their spot. They used to meet up here to take a break from work, talk about their futures, and get away from all the drama that came with being a Firebrand. Meeting here at the rock after not seeing each other for the past eleven years brought back a whole batch of good memories.

But something in Vaughn's voice had warned this reunion wouldn't be a party. And that same something had sent a cold chill racing down Hudson's back.

To READ MORE about Hudson and find out if the Firebrand family can finally mend fences and unite, click here.

ALSO BY BARB HAN

Texas Firebrand

Rancher to the Rescue

Disarming the Rancher

Rancher under Fire

Rancher on the Line

Undercover with the Rancher

Rancher in Danger

Set-up with the Rancher

Rancher under the Gun

Taking Cover with the Rancher

Don't Mess With Texas Cowboys

Texas Cowboy's Protection

Texas Cowboy Justice

Texas Cowboy's Honor

Texas Cowboy Daddy

Texas Cowboy's Baby

Texas Cowboy's Bride

Texas Cowboy's Family

Cowboys of Cattle Cove

Cowboy Reckoning

Cowboy Cover-up

Cowboy Retribution

Cowboy Judgment

Cowboy Conspiracy

Cowboy Rescue

Cowboy Target

Cowboy Redemption

Cowboy Intrigue

Cowboy Ransom

Crisis: Cattle Barge

Sudden Setup

Endangered Heiress

Texas Grit

Kidnapped at Christmas

Murder and Mistletoe

Bulletproof Christmas

For more of Barb's books, visit www.BarbHan.com.

ABOUT THE AUTHOR

Barb Han is a USA TODAY and Publisher's Weekly Best-selling Author. Reviewers have called her books "heartfelt" and "exciting."

Barb lives in Texas—her true north—with her adventurous family, a poodle mix and a spunky rescue who is often referred to as a hot mess. She is the proud owner of too many books (if there is such a thing). When not writing, she can be found exploring Manhattan, on a mountain either hiking or skiing depending on the season, or swimming in her own backyard.

Sign up for Barb's newsletter at www.BarbHan.com.

Printed in Great Britain
by Amazon